AN END TO AUTUMN

AN END TO AUTUMN

by

IAIN CRICHTON SMITH

LONDON
VICTOR GOLLANCZ LTD
1978

ISBN 0 575 02563 8

Printed in Great Britain by
The Bowering Press Ltd
Plymouth and London

ACKNOWLEDGEMENT

The author would like to thank the Scottish Arts
Council whose grant made it possible for him to buy
the time to write this book

PART ONE

PART ONE

TOM MALLOW PUT down the copy of *The Waste Land* which he had been glancing through before his lesson with the Sixth Year the following morning and said: "It worries me a bit."

His wife who was sitting opposite him on the sofa rereading *Jane Eyre* as she did once every year asked, without looking up, "What worries you?"

"Her coming."

It bothered him that from year to year his knowledge of *The Waste Land* seemed to be diminishing, the allusions more fragmentary and esoteric, the ideas more and more remote, the poetry, in fact, fading down roads which he would never travel again. Yet it was supposed to be a great poem: and for that matter he thought he knew it.

"It will be all right," Vera assured him, still intent on her book. "If we are all reasonable, and I don't see why we shouldn't be."

It was reasonable that they shouldn't have any children: they had worked that out between the two of them, and indeed if they had been the sort of people who liked children they probably wouldn't have married each other. There was a certain justice in the world which took care of most decisions, and they had had few enough to make. In any case they saw enough of children every day, teaching as they both did in the one school. Children, they knew, were unreasonable: they had no illusions about children though on the whole they liked them when they were outwith the house; they could be implacably selfish, but were able to be handled, preferably in large groups.

"If," echoed Tom, thinking that one of these days he would have to get hold of a Tarot pack: it surprised him that he hadn't done so yet though he was always meaning to. He thought he must have a second class mind though sometimes he considered that he had a first rate one.

Vera put down her book and said, "I don't see why we shouldn't be reasonable. She shall have her own room, her own friends if she makes any. She shall have her heating, her books, her food. I don't see why she and we shouldn't be reasonable.

When we are in school she can stay in the house or go out. She will have freedom. I don't see that there is any real problem."

In her own fierce silent way she loved Tom and wouldn't have done what she was about to do for anyone else but him.

"No," said Tom doubtfully. After all it was his own mother they were talking about and he knew her better than Vera though she probably had changed a great deal since the seven years that he had lived consistently in her house. He assumed that since she was alone and not very well her attitudes might have changed, since the prospect and experience of loneliness is supposed to concentrate the mind wonderfully, or so he had heard.

"In any case," said Vera, "nothing much is being lost. She is letting her house for six months, and if it doesn't work out she can always go back."

"That's true."

Though his wife read *Jane Eyre* she had a much clearer mind for the small things of life, he thought, than he had. Charlotte Brontë would probably have beaten Eliot in that field, though she wasn't as great a writer. Her mind at least wasn't as good, that was certain.

"That is true," he repeated. She could return to her house if things didn't work out. And that meant, he realised, that their own commitment might not be so great, since there was a clear way out of any difficulties. He wondered if his wife had considered that, and the fact that she probably had slightly worried him.

He went back to his *Waste Land* after lifting it first from the highly polished table in front of him, in which he could see the dark reflection of his own narrow composed face. He was very lucky really, and now because of the reasonableness of his wife he was being given the opportunity of bringing his mother into their home when she needed him. He felt warm and happy and grateful to Vera, whose reasonableness sometimes astonished him. For instance, unlike a great many women, she was not obsessed with property and furniture and though she liked a large house which they had, and whose mortgage they were paying together, she did not idolise the objects inside it, or at least hadn't done so up till now.

4

Also, their minds didn't clash or scrape, as happened, he had heard, with other married couples. They had settled from the beginning into a comfortable harmony, not the harmony of the spheres but a more equable terrestrial harmony where objects had their place, did not vibrate with excessive emotion or eeriness; and in which they sat down as if on chairs in front of the fire on a winter's night when outside the storm was howling.

Though really there had been few storms in his life, or for that matter in hers.

"We were quite poor," he said aloud to his wife. "We were in fact very poor." And he thought how poor after his father's death they had been. His father, a railwayman, had died quite young of cancer and he remembered that the house had been very dark and dull and gloomy for many months afterwards and that his mother had wept, suddenly and unexpectedly, for a long time, sometimes when she heard the sound of a train in the night. It occurred to him that his mother might have felt guilty for his father's death though there was no reason why she should: his father and mother hadn't quarrelled much as far as he could recall.

One night he had found his mother weeping in a darkened room by herself after he had come from playing football, and it seemed to him that her eyes showed white in the dark. He had been very frightened.

"It was God's will," she said later, "that your father died." And her mind slammed shut like a carriage door.

"Yes," he had replied, though by that time he didn't believe in God, having heard of Darwin.

His mother was a large woman with a large head and he sometimes thought she was rather stupid, for he regarded intelligence highly, perhaps because he was a teacher and met so much silliness and careless ineptitude. On the other hand she could be very passionate and emotional and had been liable to gather him suddenly in her arms when he was young.

"You've told me that before," said Vera, back at her book again.

The room was very quiet. On the wall were reproductions of some paintings by Hockney which had come from an Art Club. He had bought these with one of his sudden enthusiasms though he would never have bought books from a Book Club.

"I think," he said aloud, "that my mother was much stronger than my father. He struck me as not being very happy as a railwayman, though he used to take me down to see the trains. The funny thing is, I never wanted to be an engine driver."

He sometimes wondered whether he was not ashamed of his parents, or at least might not have been if for instance they had appeared with him in society, for a *faux pas* in conversation disturbed him very much. He was, he thought, conventional, and even in University had never been rebellious, believing that the best periods in human history had been those when there had either been a tyrant or an oligarchy. He believed strongly in moral principles such as intellectual honesty, charitableness, where it was possible, and courage.

"Don't worry," said Vera, "it will be all right." And she raised her eyes from *Jane Eyre* and stared at him with her usual cool gaze. He often wondered why she read *Jane Eyre* when she was such a reasonable person. And why she believed in horoscopes.

"I'm sure," he said. He had left his mother finally after University. From that time he had only been fitfully in her house and for only short periods.

"I was just thinking," he said to Vera, "about King Lear."

"What about King Lear?" she said.

"I was thinking that perhaps King Lear deserved something of what he got."

"I would say that was true." Her words were cool and measured, exactly chosen.

His wife Vera was very clever, he thought. She was a good cook, a good gardener (though they hadn't managed to do much with the garden as yet) and she had a good mind when she applied it; but she was, unlike him, suspicious of the abstract. Thus she had none of his interest in mathematics and science, whose ideas attracted him. He also believed, which he didn't think was the case with her, that lessons could be drawn from literature and that these in turn could be applied to life. But she was certainly a much better judge of human nature than he was and a more conscientious though, he surmised, less surprising teacher. He had a certain excessive enthusiasm in his nature which she didn't have and which he only revealed to his classes.

"The old are our responsibility," he said. "I feel that. I think that's what *King Lear* is trying to teach us, that no matter what the old are like we must look after them. No matter what."

"I'm not wholly sure about that," said Vera. "Though you may be right."

"I am," said Tom, "I think wholly sure," thinking of the storm which had blown the old king out to the moors, for it always reminded him of the storm through which his own father had driven one night, in his train, while his mother pulsed blindly at the windows like a moth, saying over and over again that something would happen to him. In fact nothing had and he had arrived safely home wondering what the fuss had been about while his mother was white-faced and in tears.

And now she was coming to stay with them in this small town and leaving Edinburgh.

"I don't think she can be all that well," he mused. "Or she wouldn't have come. Did you not think she was looking rather ill?"

"Perhaps a little," said Vera. "I thought her memory wasn't quite as good. She told us the same story twice in the one evening, if you remember."

"What story was that?"

"The one about how she met your father."

"At the dance, you mean. But still one expects that at her age. She is seventy, you know, and was rather older than my father."

"Yes."

Vera's own father was a solicitor who had spoken very little to her during her childhood so that she had found herself in a world of books into which she escaped and from which her mother, a lover of the theatre, had not bothered to extricate her. The marriage hadn't been a very suitable one for her mother had never shown the slightest interest in the law nor her father any interest in the theatre. Which was probably why he hadn't become a barrister.

Vera had therefore grown up with much suspicion about the emotions and had placed little reliance, eventually, on her mother's random protestations of love for her. She had acquired an almost nun-like air which was both remote and slightly haughty. It surprised her that she loved Tom so much, but from the beginning he had treated her as an equal which her father had never

7

done, and was willing to talk to her at great length about anything that interested him or her. She had met him in a library where she had been studying for her Honours Examination, as he also had been. They had both gone in search of the same book—a copy of Donne's poems—and had come after a while to an amicable agreement as to who would use it first.

Later they had gone to cafés together, to theatres and concerts: sometimes at weekends they had gone for long walks. She remembered especially the autumn leaves. They had discussed moral questions though she was more likely to draw on personal experience while Tom used logical arguments. One day she realised that she loved him. They were walking down a street and she saw his shadow beside hers on the stone, and the shadows walking together seemed to her symbolic of some deep relationship, some consonance, cool and inevitable. For the first time she had taken his arm and he had looked at her with surprise.

Tom was the only person with whom she had ever been out: in fact in her school which was an exclusively girls' one, in which she had to wear a lilac uniform, she had hardly ever met a male except the Music master who didn't like teaching in violent boys' schools. Her dreams had not been of boys at all but rather of some spiritual world occupied by few people and these neither girls nor boys but kind presences who showed her much affability. She liked a number of teachers in the school, especially the remote competent Miss Hales, whose aseptic perfume seemed to combine with it a nostalgic autumnal smell as of leaves. She played no games, not even hockey, and had no team spirit at all.

It would probably have surprised Tom to discover how much she relied on him for she never showed her emotions and always maintained the same equable poise. It never occurred to him that she needed him deeply, for her emotions, though controlled, ran more deeply than his. She never showed excessive feeling and though she loved books was not liable to be conquered by imagery or bravado but rather by a hopeless pathos which belonged to another world and not to this one.

The reason why she agreed to Tom's having his mother in the house was that she sensed it was important to him and not because she had any deep feelings about his mother, one way or the other. She believed that reasonableness would be enough and

8

that they could all get on together reasonably. At the back of her mind, though she was not conscious of it, was a picture of her mother-in-law quietly reading books in her room, as she herself had done in her childhood, ignoring both her father's coldness and her mother's spasmodic and undependable and yes, theatrical, affection.

In ordinary affairs Vera was surprisingly competent and she had a very shrewd mind which was not easily deceived. She was not liked but she was respected. Her pupils thought her fair and knowledgeable but she didn't generate the kind of coarse warmth which children respond to; so they gave her little of themselves, though they were never disobedient. She did not in fact require more of them, for excess of love would have made her uncomfortable. Her colleagues respected her but again did not particularly like her for there was about her an inexplicable and rather irritating air of superiority as if she were implying that she had to be with them but she didn't particularly wish to be. She didn't talk to anyone much and if she ever did she never volunteered any information about herself at all. Other more spontaneous people didn't like her for this, and thought her mean, both with her emotions and her mind.

She was clever enough to see that Tom for some reason felt guilty about his mother and would probably have done so about his father too, if he had lived. She herself had nothing against her mother-in-law, though the latter was inclined to ramble on about the old days; that, Vera supposed, was natural and to be expected. She looked around her at the comfortable room in which she and Tom were sitting, the deep black leather easy chairs which formed part of the suite which the sofa on which she was sitting completed; the sideboard, with the glasses and the crystal, which they had got at their marriage; the shelves of books which ran along one wall; the wooden-framed electric fire large enough to be considered a piece of furniture; the small table with the vase which contained artificial flowers (she would have liked real ones but they hadn't got down to the garden yet); the large windows with the bronze curtains. And she looked at Tom who was sitting in one of the black leather chairs with another small table in front of him which he used for marking exercises when he had any to mark. He was staring at his book in a puzzled manner

9

and when he appeared perplexed small lines appeared in his forehead. These for some reason displeased her for she liked smoothness, as if they reminded her of a mortality which she would have preferred to forget. She would in fact have wished to begin from the beginning with Tom, as if they were setting off on an original exclusive journey unshadowed by the past, but this was not possible for her own parents, especially her mother, would come to visit her now and again when for some reason they grew tired of Edinburgh, or her mother wished to return "to nature" and sample again "the simple life". It was fortunate that there was no theatre in the small town in which they lived.

The two of them on the whole were lucky for they succeeded in keeping themselves to themselves, they had congenial work which they liked doing, in the same place, and they did not exhaust each other with emotional demands or jealousies.

"It's a funny thing," said Tom, laying his book down, "I think I'm going off Eliot."

"Are you?" she said with genuine surprise. "And why do you think that is?"

"I don't know. When I was reading there was an image kept coming back to me. It was an image of an old fat woman I used to see walking about the street when I was young. She was a large woman with a red face and large lips and her stomach jutted out in front of her and she was always carrying a bag. But the thing was that she was talking to herself. Whenever you saw her she was holding long conversations with herself. I never found out where she lived. I think the redness of her face must have been caused by high blood pressure."

"That's odd," said Vera absently. "I wonder why that particular image comes back to you."

"I don't know. I always think of her as walking along on a windy day and her skirts are being blown about her legs which are also fat and red." Quite irrelevantly he added, "My mother doesn't read much. You remember three years ago when I took out a subscription to the *People's Friend* for her. I thought it would pass the time for her. But I don't think she ever read any of the magazines, so she told me to stop them."

"Yes, a lot of them read the *People's Friend*," said Vera as if she thought of his mother as belonging to a certain class of people, definite and fixed. "I should have thought she might have liked the stories."

"No, not at all," Tom pursued. "She said she had too much to do, and she didn't really have all that much. Certainly she worked in the garden but that was only in the mornings. She could have read in the afternoons or the evenings if she had wished, but she didn't. My father read a lot. Mostly serious books, non-fiction. I don't think he read a fiction book in his whole life. But he was always reading about the pyramids or about foreign countries. He wasn't at all political: he only read for information."

"Well, at least she will have a TV set in her room," said Vera. "She can watch that if she feels bored."

She herself didn't watch the TV much, and in fact only did so when there was a play on which she had asked her pupils to see, one whose text they were studying in school and which would help them in the examinations. Now and again however she would also watch documentaries about famous composers such as Schoenberg, for she was very fond of music and liked to know biographical facts, feeling that knowledge of the lives of creative people was important to an understanding of their work. Tom was more interested in painting than he was in music, though his knowledge was sporadic and amateurish.

Vera looked out through the window ahead of her. It was an autumn evening and the landscape looked brown. Already in late August she felt a strange bitter nostalgia as she always did at that time of year as if something was saying goodbye to her, as if some slant light were crossing the bare land. At twenty-seven she did not really feel old: for that matter she couldn't remember a time when she had felt young either. What she sometimes felt was the strain of being herself, of holding herself tightly in the necessary check, of not giving anything away. People regarding her might find there an enviable coolness which was more worked for than many of them realised. Days passed and certainly they passed in tranquillity, for Tom and she hardly ever quarrelled. Tranquillity she judged was better than its opposite however it contained its own terrors, however it spoke of absence.

"Well," said Tom finally shutting his book, "that's it. I'm sure that I still don't know a quarter of what it's about but it will

11

have to do. Would you like a cup of tea? I'll go and make one."

"Yes. That would be fine."

He went off to the kitchen as he always did at about that time of night, and she was left alone. Sometimes, she thought, she liked being alone, even free of Tom, just for a while. She wondered if he ever felt like that: he certainly never said so. But then of course there were certain subjects which one simply did not discuss. She considered that she might survive alone for a certain time, but wasn't sure whether she might survive for long. Perhaps Tom might survive better than her. One mused about things like that sometimes, or rather they swam into one's head without warning.

Neither of them of course was a dreamer. Tom had done quite a lot of work on the house in the way of painting and shelf-building and she had helped him: for instance she had chosen, and put up the wallpaper, for Tom was very impatient of exact measurement, in which however she believed. Her teaching was far less spontaneous than Tom's and more meticulously prepared. She was also better than he was with the more difficult classes. She didn't allow them much scope: but on the whole she preferred the others.

Tom came in and laid the tray down on the table. He had brought some biscuits which they ate.

As they sat there in the room, the only sound being that of the yellow flaring bird-shaped wall clock which her mother had given them, they felt in complete harmony with their surroundings and with each other. It was an achieved ease in which they lived, or so they thought. To Tom her cool classical figure, her pale narrow face with the fair hair combed flowingly away from the head, seemed exactly what he wanted: or at least that was what he thought more often than not.

And to her Tom was exactly what she wanted though she did not think of his physical presence much. She rested in his care and from that safety set out on her cold and otherwise self-sufficient voyage.

2

QUITE EARLY ON the Saturday Tom took his car down to the railway station and waited inside it for a while. It was a cool, calm morning and from where he was parked he could see a train waiting though as he didn't use trains he didn't know whether it was about to go or not. The station of course was much smaller than the one to which his father had used sometimes to take him, introducing him once, with a mixture of servility and pride, to the stationmaster, an apparently busy little man with a toothbrush moustache who had given him a hard white sweet. In that station there had been a continual pulsation of steam, a rushing of people, a pushing of cases by porters, a sense of a whole world in continual motion. Sometimes he felt that he could take a train somewhere, anywhere, to find a series of different landscapes and end up perhaps in Arabia or Turkey or even in fabulous Athens. But of course he had never done that. Because his father had worked on the railways they had been given free travel, but they had never been adventurous and had stayed inside Scotland. The radiation of rails had attracted him but he had stayed where he was and his life had been one of careful uneventfulness: his wife told him that since he was a Capricorn unadventurousness was to be expected of him.

He liked the small town in which he lived but sometimes, as in his youth, he felt a phantasmal motion of departure, especially on hazy summer mornings, as if he were a child again in a busy railway station. What was it he wanted that he didn't have? He often wondered and couldn't think of anything. After all he was happy in his work, he had a good home and a very agreeable wife, and his surroundings were themselves beautiful, a fine blending of sea and land. What therefore was he looking for on those days, for he only felt those motions of departure at certain times and not constantly. He was sure that his wife didn't feel restless, or if she did she never revealed it in any way, and never talked about it. She seemed to have a deeper calm than he had. Perhaps it was because she had not been brought up in an atmosphere of trains and railway stations, bound to timetables as his father, and therefore he and his mother, had been. When he was young he remembered his father waving flags from a train that was setting off into an unimaginable country and which would never return no matter how hard he ran after it and pleaded with his father to wait. In the end of course, his father had done just that, he had set off on a final journey and hadn't returned. The rails had been narrow and he had finally turned a corner from which one could see only steam like breath arising and being dissipated on the chilly air.

Tom sat for a while in the car thinking, and now and again letting his gaze rest on the present, on the fishing boats that he could see in the harbour, on the hills that he could see on the other side of the bay. What a beautiful little town it was, with its changing lights so different from the hard definite rigid light of Edinburgh which delineated so firmly massive stone buildings such as insurance offices. Here the light broke randomly on water and stone, in a less assured and more wavering manner but at nights flared into the most theatrical sunsets such as his mother-in-law, he thought wryly, might have disported herself in.

As he waited for the train bearing his mother to come into the station, he had a strange feeling that something decisive was going to happen, though he didn't know what it was. It was true, as Vera had surmised, that he felt guilty about his mother though there was no particular reason why he should. In a certain sense his guilt was literary, as if he saw himself as a character in a book who had left his own class and was bound therefore to feel guilty. By attending university he had placed a distance between himself and his father whose untrained though industrious mind was as inferior to his own as an old-fashioned adding machine to a modern computer. The image of his father in his not very attractive and slightly blurred blue uniform arose in his mind as one he felt he ought to be guilty about.

Thinking these thoughts he watched with fascination a seagull that was standing splay-clawed on the pier, turning its head from side to side, and opening its beak as if it were yawning. Perhaps if he had pulled down the window he would have found that it was screaming, Tom thought wryly. Now and again the seagull would peck at some wrecked bones, probably those of herring, that lay on the stone. Tom could see its stony eyes even from the

14

inside of the car, a good distance away. The seagull seemed to him to be an image of self-containment, concerned only with its food, its eye cold and remote, and it was as if he was possessed by a sudden blind hatred of the bird, such that if people hadn't been about he might have thrown a stone at it. But in fact he only looked at his watch to find that there were another ten minutes to go before the train came in.

He got out of the car, leaving it unlocked for nothing was likely to happen to it, and walked slowly into the station. There were one or two pupils at the bookstall glancing through magazines about football and he nodded to them absently and they smiled back with the sort of smile that they offered when they were not actually in school. He strolled on to the gate through which his mother would appear when she came, and stood there, a slightly hunched figure, gazing along the rails as if they were double-barrelled shotguns aimed from the haze towards him.

Eventually the train wormed itself into the station and he watched as door after door opened, and people stepped out onto the platform. Then he saw her and with a sudden rush he went towards her for she was looking around in a bewildered manner, almost as if she were in a foreign country whose language she did not know. She had a large black case which a tall man with a briefcase was helping her with, but when he saw Tom coming he nodded briefly and walked briskly towards the exit. She was wearing a black hat and black coat as if she was still in mourning, helpless and confused. He took the case from her and they walked towards the exit side by side, he slowing down to accommodate his pace to hers. He never kissed her when they met, though his mother-in-law kissed him with a dramatic flourish each time he met her, as if he had just arrived from the North Pole, and she might never see him again if she didn't greet him quickly.

"Did you have a good journey?" he asked and found that his voice was slightly colder than he would have wished.

"Yes," she said, "I was talking to a woman who was coming here on holiday. She's from England and she comes every year. She says she likes it very much."

"Yes, we get a lot of tourists," said Tom who did not at that time think of himself as a tourist. "Have the people moved into the house?"

"They moved in yesterday. Very nice people. He's a chartered accountant and she doesn't work. They've got a lovely little girl. She's only five and she's just gone to school."

"You'll like it here," said Tom. "Plenty of sea, plenty of fresh air. You can come and sit in the gardens in the warm weather, and it'll pass the time for you." And he pointed out to her the railed-in garden, with the benches on each side of it, on which even then some tourists were sitting, a number of them reading newspapers.

"It is lovely," she said and certainly the town was looking its best on that fine autumn morning, the flowers still in bloom, the sea calm and sparkling, and the islands green in the distance. It was as if she were coming on a holiday and not to stay, for nowhere could she see the sort of cramped tenements to which she had been used in her youth. It was as if she were gazing at a picture, staged and perfect, distant and yet slightly faked.

"Lovely," she repeated. "Where is your school?"

"It's not near here. We won't actually be passing it," he said taking out his key to open the boot of the car in order to put the case in.

"That Englishwoman was saying that she comes every year. She said she wouldn't go anywhere else for her holidays."

He thought she was trying to put him at his ease, and she thought that he was looking thin and worried. Perhaps he was working too hard.

"Are you well?" he asked. "Are you quite well?"

"I'm not bad," she replied. "I sometimes have a slight dizziness but not much. The doctor said there wasn't anything really wrong. He said my lungs are still very good for a person of my age."

And she laughed a little for she liked the doctor, a young man who joked with her when he came to visit.

He opened the car door for her and waited till she had settled herself in the seat. As they drove off he felt as if he were bringing home a conquest, a treasure of some kind, and it made him feel happy so that as he indicated to her the various features and buildings, they appeared as personal gifts which it was in his power to grant. He heard himself saying to her, "I used to worry about you down there, with all that vandalism. You haven't had any more break-ins?"

"No, just the one," she said. "You have a lot of trees here."

"Yes," he answered as if they belonged to him.

When they drew up at the door of the large house, Vera was standing there as if she had been waiting and watching for them. She came forward and as her mother-in-law stepped slightly awkwardly from the car she kissed her lightly on the forehead as if she were giving her the sort of kiss a nun might give.

"I hope you haven't had a tiring journey."

"No it was quite nice," said her mother-in-law. Vera waited for Tom to get the case out of the boot and then, Tom preceding them, she and Mrs Mallow entered the house.

Vera took Mrs Mallow into the living room and said to Tom when he had come in after depositing the case, "Your mother can go to her room later. I think we should have a cup of coffee now. Would you like that?" she asked her mother-in-law, helping her to remove her coat and hat and leaving them for the time being on a hook behind the living-room door.

"Yes I would, thank you," said Mrs Mallow, sinking deeply into the sofa. "I was telling Tom that I met an Englishwoman who told me that she always came here on holiday. Her husband is a professor but he's too busy to come with her."

"A professor of what?" said Vera handing the cups round.

"I don't know. Was it science? I can't remember. They had been married for thirty years, she told me."

She sipped the coffee and looked around her, not as yet feeling at home, and watching Tom who was glancing at the headlines of the morning paper but who, realising that she was staring at him, put it down again and said to Vera:

"She tells me that she gets a little dizziness now and again."

"Oh nothing much, nothing to worry about," his mother protested. "Not often. Only once or twice when I was shopping. It wasn't anything. I was telling Tom that the doctor said that I had good lungs. He told me I had the lungs of a sixteen-year-old."

"That's good," said Vera. "I'm sure neither Tom nor I have that," and her mother-in-law laughed.

"I think I have the lungs of a ninety-year-old," said Tom. "We don't get enough exercise. We should take more exercise."

"It's a lovely house," said his mother. "A lovely house."

"Is the coffee sweet enough," Vera asked.

"Yes, yes, it's good coffee. Exactly as I like it," though in fact it was not quite as sweet as she usually wanted it.

"I hope you haven't had any more break-ins."

"No no, just the one. And they didn't take anything. Of course I don't have much anyway. I mean I don't have any jewellery or anything like that."

"They wouldn't get much jewellery here either," said Tom, "though you don't get many break-ins in this place. Or at least hardly ever. Shops maybe but houses hardly ever. You won't need to worry about that."

"Well, that's a relief. Are you sure you haven't something to do? I'm not keeping you back or anything?"

"Not at all," they both said simultaneously.

"Not at all. We don't do much work on a Saturday. Hardly any really. But if you would like to see your room," Vera suggested.

"I don't mind," her mother-in-law replied and Vera and Tom went along with her.

As he stood outside the door of the room with his mother, Vera behind him, Tom had the strangest feeling as if he were a warder showing a prisoner into his cell, and yet there was no reason why he should, since the room was in fact a very fine one with large windows looking out on to the hills and trees at the back, and was furnished neatly with a TV set, an electric fire, a bed with a yellow continental quilt, a wardrobe and basketwork chair. There was also a dressing table of the same light contemporary wood as the wardrobe with a large mirror above it. The curtains were a pale yellow.

"This is your room, mother," he said, using the word for the first time.

"It's lovely," she said enthusiastically. "Lovely. It's so airy and light."

And indeed it was airy and light and sunny. There was about it no sense of sweat or time, its wood was innocent and clear, no deep thoughts had ever brooded in it, the windows and furniture were all without memory.

She stood there as if not quite believing that the room belonged

18

to her, as if she were a lodger moving in, as if she would at any moment ask them what the terms might be, or when breakfast would be served in the morning. Tom laid her case down in the middle of the room and said rapidly, "Put on the TV any time you like. And don't worry about the electric fire. Use it as much as you like. Remember it is your room. If there's anything else you want, you ask."

"If the quilt isn't warm enough," Vera added, "just tell me. But we usually find that these quilts are warm enough on their own without blankets."

"Well then," said Tom awkwardly, "we'll leave you just now. The bathroom is on the left as you leave the room. We'll leave you then," he said again. He and Vera left the room, the door still open. He didn't say anything: it was as if in that moment, in that encounter, his mind had been flooded with images from the past, they all swam on the sea of his fresh feeling, images from tenement rooms in a big city, massive brown wardrobes, sideboards huge and becalmed, ponderous chairs, flowered wallpaper, speckled ceilings inadequately whitewashed.

A train long and brown, a sinuous snake, bulleted through the walls, and turned into a coffin and then he was standing in a gush of feeling at his father's grave. The day was clear and warm. The minister was standing at the graveside speaking of the Resurrection and the Life, and the many mansions to which all the mourners were invited. He himself waited, hearing above the words the hum of a wasp about his head, for the moment when he would be summoned to take a cord of the coffin and help lower it into the grave. All around him he saw the intent faces of the mourners, many of them blinking their eyes rapidly, and they seemed to him like the faces he had seen in a painting by Rubens or some other painter (was it Rembrandt?), permanent, puzzled, austere.

Then he was called and he stepped forward. He stood there looking down into the open grave, feeling slightly dizzy as if he might fall into it, following the small light body of his diminished father. It was as if he and his father had entered a tunnel through which the train would eventually emerge into bright daylight. But he knew that this would not happen. And as the coffin swayed down on its ropes, he woke up and there beside him, standing slightly perplexed, was Vera and across his face passed

19

a shade. Suddenly he put his hand in hers and without saying anything squeezed it slightly and went back into the living room. They stood there in the common light, he more disturbed than she for some reason that he could not put a name to till he realised that the funeral he was remembering could not have been his father's at all, since he had been too young to attend it.

He tried to think whose funeral it could have been, but couldn't remember. She gathered the coffee cups together to wash them and in front of him still on the table was his copy of *The Waste Land*.

3

ON THE FOLLOWING morning Mrs Mallow woke early, the sun pouring through the window, and all around her an unaccustomed silence, except for the cry of seagulls. She felt light and free and happy as if she had thrown the weight of life's responsibility on others, and had only to follow her own desires. She dressed rapidly after she had been to the bathroom—where she had noticed on top of the cistern a doll with flaxen hair and very clear blue eyes—and then finding that the other two were not yet up, she sat in her room for a while, thinking that she did not want to go out in case she disturbed them. She also left the electric fire unlit lest she should waste too much electricity, which had become so expensive in recent months.

Her journey to her son's house had been a response to his repeated suggestions after her own house had been broken into one evening when she had been in church. She had thought of keeping it from him but had not in fact done so for the rather odd reason that it had given her something to tell him when he had visited her, since he believed that she led an uneventful life. The burglars had forced a back window and had taken the small radio which he had given her, as well as a few ornaments, and a clock: there was little else of value in the house. Perhaps because of this they had scattered some documents, including insurance policies, on the floor, and had left the lock of the window smashed. For the first time since she had lived in the house she had felt vulnerable. At first she hadn't known what to do but had finally decided to phone for the police who came along, had a look at the room, advised her to have the window lock repaired, took a list of the stuff that had been taken (she didn't know what make the radio had been) and then left her without much hope that she would ever get any of it back. Tom had been incensed when she had told him about it, as if he had been personally threatened. He had stormed down to the police station, and had been very rude to them: and then he had come back and told her that she must come and stay with him and Vera.

She hadn't actually thought of that before, though she had

wondered what would become of her if she was unable to look after herself. She only thought of this in a vague sort of way and not constantly. She was a rather heavy, big-boned woman and sometimes when she was out shopping, especially among traffic, she felt moments of dizziness as if her body were becoming too large to handle, and also more vague than it had been before. She found too that the world was becoming rather remote, and sometimes had the odd feeling that people were laughing at her and talking behind her back. Her only recreation, if it could be called that, was church. In church she relaxed in a restful silence, different from the silence that surrounded her at home; she could only think of it as a holy silence. Her troubles and torments seemed to fade away, leaving her mind and body light and fresh. Even the smell of the varnished seats conforted her, and sometimes in spring and summer she would look at the small high windows and see beyond them the motion of new green leaves.

As she was thinking these thoughts she heard movement in the house and knew that either Tom or Vera or both were up. She glanced at her tiny watch and noticed that the time was nine o'clock. She wondered if it would be possible for her to go to church. It was strange to be in somebody else's house, even though it was her son's: she had never been in a house before that wasn't her own or her husband's. The first one had been a flat in a tenement and now there was the small semi-detached house which she had rented out for a few months. It was odd to be waiting on the pleasure of others, and to adapt to their routine which would probably be very different from her own. It was strange that there should have been a doll in the bathroom when there were no children in the house, and it looked very much as if there wouldn't be any. A house with children was different, there was a sense of life, laughter, noise, quarrelling. But there was a clean silence about this house as if it had not yet wakened up, as if everything rested securely in its place and would remain so. She quite liked her daughter-in-law or, rather, didn't dislike her, but she had great difficulty in speaking to her and felt rather frightened of her in a way.

By ten o'clock she smelt bacon frying, and prepared to go into the living room but then decided against it. She thought her son

22

would come to the door which in fact he eventually did. Casually dressed in a green jersey he seemed in good humour.

"Did you sleep well?" he asked.

"Like a log," she said.

"That's good. Would you like to come into the living room? You should have put the fire on."

"I'm warm enough," she answered, for she did feel warm or at least not cold. He seemed surprised to find her already dressed in her brown dress with the brooch at the throat, rather as if he had expected to find her in a dressing-gown.

She followed him into the living room and he left her, as he said, to go for the papers. Vera came out of the kitchen to say good morning and then went back to her cooking. From the window she could see the sea through a veil of trees which were already turning brown. Tom had once taken her on holiday after he had started working and before his marriage and they had stayed in a hotel, and she felt now as she had felt then, when they were waiting at the table for breakfast, the red napkins folded in front of them, the white cloth on the table, the grapefruit in the glass. "I feel so stupid," she thought, "I have brought them my stupidity." But she was comforted by the fact that she could always go back to her own house. After all she had only rented it out for six months and didn't need to renew the lease if she didn't want to.

Vera finally came in with the bacon and eggs, and laid them on the table. "Can I help you?" said her mother-in-law.

"No," said Vera, "that will be all right. You sit there and rest."

At the same time Mrs Mallow would have preferred to help her, for deep within her was the soul of the servant: in fact she would have been happy to be a maid, for that would have given her a place, but of course that was impossible. Before her marriage she had done work like that, she had been a waitress, and she had been very happy in her work: she remembered that time as happy and joyous and full of laughter. She didn't think that Vera had ever done anything like that, or at least she would be very surprised if she found that she had. For a moment she had a brief intuition of those days, of beds being made, of girls shouting and throwing pillows at each other, of breathless rushing and pushing among the foam of white linen, and her face changed and became young again. Then Tom was back with the papers. He had in fact forgotten that his mother might wish to go to church for to him Sunday had become a day when he read the *Observer* and the *Sunday Times*, or rather when he and Vera read both papers alternately. His first action was to remove the business section from the *Sunday Times* and throw it into the waste-paper basket, after which he would read the news section, followed by the part which contained the book reviews, television and theatre notices. Though he didn't watch much television or for that matter ever saw any plays he read all the reviews carefully as did Vera. He felt, though he was far from London, a responsibility to keep up with what was going on. However, this morning out of a greater responsibility to his mother he didn't actually start to read the papers, and because of this he felt a slight constraint as if she were coming between him and a way of life which he had created over the years. And immediately afterwards he felt guilty that he should have such a sense of restraint at all.

As they sat at breakfast it was Vera who wondered if her mother-in-law wished to go to church and Mrs Mallow was immediately grateful to her. Yes, she did wish to go: perhaps she could walk?

"No, no," said Tom, "not at all. The church is too far away. I shall take you in the car." He couldn't remember when he had been in church last: he was not an atheist nor did he even consider himself an agnostic, he was simply indifferent. He would read theological books now and again, but he would never go to church. He felt no actual hostility towards it, it seemed to be a mediaeval out-dated institution, slightly comic and absurd, which perhaps at one time had served a useful purpose and had a certain aesthetic value but not any more. Vera was less indifferent but didn't go either. If the church had been St Giles, massive, historical, a hive of music, she might have gone, but the churches in the small town where she now lived did not attract her. They seemed to her to be small, too sociable, and lacking in resonance and true divinity. Her image of the church was one of a chaste holiness, cool and devoted to a cool and reasonable god, who liked music but did not permit excesses.

"I like going to church," said Mrs Mallow. "I always went in Edinburgh."

"Yes?" said Vera.

"Though I must say that the church isn't what it used to be," Mrs Mallow continued. "There are too many gimmicks." She used the word "gimmicks" with a certain daring as if she felt it was not quite her sort of word. She was finding it difficult to make conversation for neither Tom no Vera seemed to talk much. In the past she had been used to people who talked a lot, who brought news home to her, who watched the little details of the world and were interested in them. Neither Tom nor Vera was like that at all: for instance they never mentioned events at the school to her. Their silences, she thought, might oppress her but at the same time she accepted that that was how they were. Still, she was looking forward to going to church, in a new town, and on such a fine morning and she felt slightly excited and even apprehensive.

"Your church is in Victoria Street," Vera told her. "It's a fairly large church. What's the name of the minister, Tom?"

"Haven't a clue. It isn't Munro, is it? I seem to recall some-one called Munro. A small man with a moustache who goes about on a bicycle."

"I don't think so. I've a feeling it's some other name."

"Well," said Tom, "my mother will find out in due time. It may come to her as a magnificent surprise." This last joke had come out of the blue and he laughed loudly, though his mother didn't laugh at all. He had a habit of coming out with such springing witticisms from a superfluousness of high spirits that overflowed often in the mornings: and after he had said them he would burst out into sudden laughter. Neither Vera nor his mother, he thought, had a sense of the absurd. Tom, on the other hand, had a vision of a small minister in a white cloak appearing as if by miracle in front of his mother and presenting her with a grandiloquent name, his hands folded equably on a bible. He ate his bacon and egg contentedly.

"Have you any idea when the service starts?" Vera asked.

"Not the foggiest. Will it not be in the local rag? Oh, sorry, we threw it out didn't we? You haven't seen our local paper yet," he said to his mother. "That is another treat in store for you."

Vera looked at him in a puzzled manner as if she thought he was acting strangely and his mother said, "It will be about eleven, I should think. It won't be earlier than eleven. Sometimes half past but usually eleven. In Edinburgh it is eleven, though you have to be there before." The words came from her in a rush, for she was on her own home ground, she was contributing facts of which she was sure.

"I'm sure that will be right," said Tom. It occurred to him to wonder what Vera thought of his mother. Maybe she considered her dull and dim, which she in effect was, though on the other hand she had her own virtues. He didn't like her going on in this remorselessly factual way about trivial things and sometimes she embarrassed him, though he felt he ought not to be embarrassed. His mother however wasn't finished yet.

"The attendance in our church is going down. It's mostly women now. Hardly any of the men go. You see them working in their gardens or playing golf." She stopped as if she had found herself talking about a church which was of a higher class than it had actually been. Her own friends, or at least the women she talked to when she went to church, weren't high class at all. They were ordinary women whose husbands had very ordinary jobs.

"Well," said Tom, "if you're ready."

"I'll get my coat," said his mother and she went to her room from which she soon returned dressed to go out. Tom had by this time gone to the car and in a short while she was sitting beside him. It was a nice green car which she liked, and she was happy to be with him. After all he was her own son, she had reared him, and now he had a good job and was quite successful. She was proud of him. She even longed to touch him, to straighten the collar of his jersey, but didn't dare to do so: he looked so confident and negligent. Never again would she touch him as she had done when he was young, when he had suffered the turmoils of boyhood and youth, when he had the illnesses common to children, when he had seemed so alone and helpless. It was she however who was now the child and he who was setting out into the wide world. Nevertheless she wished that he would go to church.

The car, almost like a taxi which she had hired, drew up outside the church, the doors of which were open wide revealing

26

the elders like butlers in black suits waiting with hymn books in their hands like salvers, and smiling genially on all who came in, sometimes bending down deferentially to listen to what someone had to say. Tom leaned over and opened the door of the car for her and watched her as she went towards the church, feeling a strange vexation, as if he were allowing her to set out without help on an adventure which he could not take part in because his mind was hostile to it. For he could not bring himself to go to church, and yet why shouldn't he? Was his mother less important to him than the integrity of his own mind? He watched her, a stranger, approaching the open door: he saw an elder offering her a hymn book, and then she went into the church in her black coat and disappeared. It was like himself going to school for the first time and his mother watching him, no longer able to go with him, having grown too old, however she might wish to be with him.

He sat in the car for a long time thinking, for it seemed to him that even this simple action of taking his mother to church and then leaving her at the door was important, was indeed of the greatest importance. The pathos of it disturbed him, so that he felt pity for his mother who was now sitting on her own among strangers, dependent wholly on the furniture and the language of the church itself, on its continuity and its resonance.

Finally he turned the car away and drove home. When he went into the house Vera was reading the *Observer*. She raised her head briefly and said to him:

"I suppose it has occurred to you that you'll have to collect your mother later." As a matter of fact it hadn't occurred to him and he felt obscurely angry both at himself and at Vera.

"It hadn't," he said tersely. She looked up at him in surprise as if something in his tone troubled her, but he turned to the *Sunday Times* and to the book page. He spent some time trying to understand the first sentence of a review of a book about psychology, and then glanced up from the paper and looked around him. He couldn't see Vera behind the *Observer* which was held up in front of her like the open marble bible in a churchyard. There was a smell of cooking from the kitchen, the clock on the wall ticked irritatingly, the print by Hockney stared down at him.

He turned back to the *Sunday Times*, concentrating on the article with great intensity, and feeling that he was fighting against some preoccupation which he couldn't identify, but at the same time determined to finish reading the papers before he went to collect his mother. The two of them read in silence except that once Tom said, "I hope she will like the church," and Vera as if completely understanding his thought said, "I hope so too.' '

4

BEFORE LEAVING FOR school, Vera got into the habit of taking a light breakfast to her mother-in-law in her bedroom, and the latter rose after they had left. She found the house even more silent than her own since it was well away from the noise of traffic. At times she even thought of entering their bedroom to see what it was like, but confined herself to the living room, her own room, the bathroom, the kitchen and the dining room, and another spare bedroom which was as yet only sparsely furnished. The house had an almost spartan newness about it, lacking the clutter of ornaments in her own house, lacking, she thought, any warmth or colour, but giving an impression of whites and yellows and a plentitude of new wood. She could find no photographs, not even wedding ones: it was as if her son and daughter-in-law lived in a world totally free of the past, of relations, committed only to themselves and the reality of their own lives, spare of ancestry. Everything in the house was new, as far as she could see, and had a flawless automatic air about it: she would have been happier if she had found a broken or irregular clock, a squeaking floor board, an old sink. But no, there was none of these. It occurred to her that perhaps they had few if any friends, and that from choice rather than necessity. There were many books all of which seemed far beyond her, even if she had been a more voracious reader. There was a garden which as yet wasn't in good order, and she thought that perhaps later she might help with that, though she wasn't an especially good gardener. Outside the house there was a bench on which she could sit if she wanted.

The two of them had told her that she could make her own light dinner if she wanted to as they wouldn't be coming back for it, since it was more convenient for them to take their lunch in school. Thus for a good part of the day she was monarch of all she surveyed, and she found this both disquieting and liberating. She wondered too if she should approach them with regard to paying them some money. On Tuesdays she would have to go to the Post Office for her pension. She didn't think that Tom would take any money from her but at least she wished to make the offer lest they should wonder why she hadn't thought of it. The problems began to proliferate as she wandered about the house or sat in the living room. Throwing oneself on the mercy of others, surrendering one's responsibility for oneself wasn't so easy as one might at first think. In Edinburgh it had appeared simple enough, as if all she had to do was to take the train, enter their house and relax. But the reality was different. The reality was that the house was a certain distance from the town, not much, but not all that central: and that her freedom was very great indeed. She decided that she would go out, and this raised another problem, for what was she to do about a key? She agonised about this for a while and then resolved that as they had told her that there was no likelihood of the house being broken into she could probably afford to leave the door off the snib: she would get a key that night. The other possibility was to snib the door and stay down town till they returned from school which she assumed would be shortly after four o'clock. But on balance it seemed to her better to leave the door unlocked, since she didn't think that she would be able to stay down town till four o'clock.

She dressed not in her black coat but in her brown one and left the house walking briskly down the brae to the road in the cool air of the morning. She noticed that at the foot of the brae was a bus stop but decided not to wait for a bus, though she was glad that she had established that buses did run past the house: a bus would be useful on rainy days or when she felt tired. By the time she had reached the town she felt quite adventurous again and was delighted by its simple attractiveness. She walked to the pier and had a look at the boxes of fish, the fishing boats with their tangle of pointed masts, the seagulls in squabbling rings in the bay. Out in the distance she could see an island, long and green, with houses on it. The sun sparkled on the water, the smell of brine was in her nostrils, and the air was clear and clean and pure.

After she had seen the pier she had a walk among the shops, buying nothing except a cake which she thought might be useful for the house. She found the atmosphere of the town relaxing as if people had all the time in the world, as if they were able to converse with each other without pressure or strain. A man who was cleaning the roads and piling withered leaves into a barrow said good morning to her. The quality of the light attracted her, it seemed softer and more restful than that of Edinburgh, and it appeared to make the houses soft yet clear. The air too was blander than the cold piercing air of Edinburgh.

After she had walked about the town for a while she decided that she would do what Tom had suggested and sit on a bench in the railed garden in the square. She opened the gate and walked in and sat down. Beside her on the bench was a woman with a shopping bag: she was slightly bow-legged and had varicose veins. She hadn't been sitting long when the woman spoke to her. It seemed to her that she had seen the woman before, perhaps in church: or it might be that she was confusing her with someone she had seen in Edinburgh, for she found, strangely enough that as she walked along the street she met people who reminded her of ones whom she had known or met in Edinburgh.

"It's a nice day," said the woman. "And it's a relief to have a seat."

"Yes," said Mrs Mallow, "isn't it?"

The woman had small birdlike eyes and what might have been a slightly Irish accent. She was in fact the sort of woman that Mrs Mallow might well have met in the early days of her marriage when she was living in a tenement in Edinburgh and for this reason she was immediately attracted to her as if she recalled to her days when she had been thoughtlessly happy, and the world had been open and free, and also full of bustle and noise. She relaxed, almost visibly.

"Do you come from here?" she asked.

"I've been living here for forty years or so. You could say I belonged here. I stay on my own, though: that's why I come down here so often. My husband's dead and my sons are all away. What about yourself?"

The woman had a brisk, direct manner of speaking which Mrs Mallow liked, and she was unusually talkative as she told her why she herself now lived in the town.

"My sons have asked me to go and live with them too," said the woman as if she and Mrs Mallow had suddenly become involved in a competition, "but I won't go except for holidays. One of my sons is a manager of a shop in England, and I've got another son in the Army. I used to stay with the one in England

31

for a while. As a matter of fact, I was down there last summer, but I don't like the wife. She and I don't get on." She shut her lips like a purse and stared fiercely ahead of her. It seemed that she would have been quite willing to wring the necks of the tall, foreign-looking flowers.

"Of course," she said, "it may be something wrong with me too. I've got my own ways and she's got hers and that's the way it is. She wouldn't make me porridge in the mornings and I like my porridge. She told me I could make it myself if I wanted to. She goes out to work and I don't believe in that. She should stay at home and look after the children—they've got three lovely children. Give me the old-fashioned woman any time, but these ones nowadays are all skin and bones and all they want to do is go out to the pubs and drink gin or vodka. I never went out when my children were growing up."

"Well I'm quite happy," Mrs Mallow insisted loyally. "I have my own room and I come and go when I please."

"They say that the day looks fine first thing in the morning," said the woman mysteriously, and then, "What does your son do?" She said. "My name's Mrs Murphy by the way. Pleased to meet you."

"My son is a teacher in the school," said Mrs Mallow rather proudly, "and so is my daughter-in-law. You might know them."

"Oh, I don't know their names now. In the old days when my sons were going to school I knew all their names and their nicknames too, and some queer ones they had. But I don't know them now. I don't know what they tell them in these schools now. The teachers are as young as the scholars, and the scholars won't get off the pavement for you. They walk down there five at a time, shouting and screaming and they push you into the gutter. The girls are just as bad as the boys. Is it only one son you have then?"

"Yes. My husband died when he was young."

"Well," said Mrs Murphy shifting her buttocks on the seat, "my people are in Ireland but I haven't seen them for thirty years. The last time I was in Ireland it was thirty years ago, come August. My husband came from Connemara. But I don't know anyone there any more. Your sons leave you and they marry and they're not the same, whatever anyone says. They may look

32

the same," and she nodded her small brisk head vigorously, "but they're not the same. They change. My son who's in the Army—he's married too, to a woman from Germany—goes all over the world. He's never brought me a matchstick though he's been all over the world. He's a Lance Corporal now."

A man who might have been the gardener passed with a rake in his hand and she shouted at him, "Great day for the flowers, Dan," and he smiled and waved back. "That's the gardener. He looks after all the gardens. Nice fellow. Tell you what," she said, "would you like a cup of tea? I get tired sitting here all the time; I've got a restless nature, you see. If you would like to come to the house for a cup of tea you'd be welcome as the flowers in May. If it wouldn't put you out of your road."

Mrs Mallow was surprised by the readiness with which she accepted the invitation, and as she walked beside the bow-legged little white-haired woman who nevertheless waddled briskly along like a sailor in rather a heavy sea, she felt quite happy as if she were setting out on a little adventure. They didn't have to walk very far for soon they came to a tenement and climbed a stair to the middle flat which had the name MURPHY on the door. Mrs Murphy took a key from a string around her neck and opened the door and Mrs Mallow found herself in a dark lobby and then in a small crowded room of the kind to which she had been used in Edinburgh. She was invited to sit down on an easy chair which had a white cloth over it, and which sat in front of a hearth empty except for newspaper and sticks.

"I'll put on the electric fire," said Mrs Murphy, and did so. "And then I'll make a cup of tea."

Left alone, Mrs Mallow looked round her. Apart from the easy chair in which she was sitting there was another one: there was also a sideboard with some photographs on it, one of a smiling young man in the uniform of a Scottish regiment, wearing a kilt and a diced cap with a badge, and the other of an older, more serious boy who looked solid and responsible, and was probably the manager, if manager he was. She also saw on the sideboard a doll-like structure which showed a crib, the Virgin Mary, a sleeping baby, and various crudely-carved animals which might have been donkeys, all painted in a garish green. And she realised that Mrs Murphy was a Catholic. It was funny that that hadn't struck her before, for she hadn't thought that there would be any Catholics in the town, apart perhaps from the Italians in the cafés: but the slightly Irish accent and the name Murphy should perhaps have warned her. She had very mixed feelings about Catholicism: on the one hand she had been brought up in a Protestant family, and on the other she had met many Catholics in the course of her life and she had liked them at least as much as she had liked the Protestants. In fact in the tenement in Edinburgh there had lived next door to her a Catholic woman from Derry who had been one of her best friends, and who every summer went over to Ireland with her asthmatic husband. One morning Mrs Mallow had pointed out to her a dirty stain on her forehead and was greatly embarrassed to learn that is was in fact meant to be there as the day was Ash Wednesday. Still, the cheap green crib was not very attractive and its vulgarity slightly upset her.

Mrs Murphy came in with two cups of tea and biscuits on a tray and sat heavily in the chair opposite her.

"I didn't ask you if you'd like any biscuits. Would you like any biscuits?"

"No, no thanks," said Mrs Mallow. "I was looking at the photographs of your sons."

"Yes. They turned out all right though they were little buggers when they were growing up. They were always shouting at each other and talking of nothing but football. I used to get sick of football. Nothing but football morning, noon and night. But I miss them now. The house feels empty. You find that too?"

"I used to," said Mrs Mallow, who was finding the tea rather sweet. "You never go to Ireland now?"

"No. I've got one or two relations there but I don't go. And anyway we lived in the back of beyond. Connemara. I don't suppose you'll know it? Nothing but big stones. I got out of it as soon as I could. No, the nights are long if your boys are away and you're without a man. I go to Mass in the mornings and most of the day in the good weather I sit on the benches, after I've done my shopping. And I've got a TV though there's nothing on it but rubbish."

"You're right there," said Mrs Mallow. "I've got TV but I never watch it."

"I'll tell you something," said Mrs Murphy, leaning back in her chair, "there's nothing for us when we grow old. We just have to get through the day and that's it. But I don't worry about it. Don't give in, that's what I always say. Don't let the buggers grind you down. Keep going, as long as you have your two legs. The people in this town are very snobbish, you know."

"Oh?"

"Very snobbish. There's the people up the hill, you know," (Mrs Mallow thought that she probably included her own son among them) "and then there's the people like us. We don't mix. They've got their Round Tables and their Rotary Clubs and the rest of it, and they wouldn't speak to you in the street. My son now isn't like that though he's a manager. And he's been abroad too. He was in Czechoslovakia and Russia and all these places and he stayed in the big hotels there. But he's friendly with his customers. It's not like that here." And she nodded her head decisively. "Would you like more tea?"

"That was fine," said Mrs Mallow. "I've had enough."

"There's plenty in the pot, you know. I always use teabags because they don't clutter up the sink. As I was saying there's them and us. Anyway, what's the point talking about it? I used to clean the stairs, that's what I did for a while. I used to go to their houses, the people up the hill, and you could hear some things there, I can tell you. You'd hear them shouting at each other, and their language was terrible. It was an education. But then they'd come to the door sweet as anything and ask you how you were. They were very mean with their money though. They never gave you anything at Christmas. Have you noticed that? It's the rich people who never give you any money. If you want help, you get it from the poor people, that's what I always say. I've noticed that all my life. They hoard it all up and then they leave thousands of pounds, and what good does it do them? They get six feet of earth in the end just like everybody else. Oh, I know them."

Mrs Mallow realised that that was true enough. The rich never did give anybody money, you were more likely to get help from the poor, that had been her own experience and most especially when her husband had died. It was the poorer neighbours who had come to sympathise with her, not the rich people, his superiors, who had worked on the railway. She hadn't seen any of them.

"You're right," she said, "I found that in Edinburgh. There was an Irishwoman who lived beside me in the tenement and she was a very nice woman. She was like a sister to me. A small woman with red cheeks and very blue eyes. She would bring me in scones that she had baked and whenever she went to Ireland she brought me back something. It might be a very small thing like a handkerchief but she always brought something back. Her husband suffered from asthma and he worked in a distillery. Sometimes he could hardly breathe."

Mrs Mallow now felt totally at ease and was talking more freely than she had done since first she came to the town. It was as if the small crowded room with its sagging chairs, its sagging sofa and its cluttered photographs had released in her a freedom which she had lost over the years, as if she breathed more relaxedly in that space signed so distinctly with the images of the past—even the Catholic ones—and as she sat there she remembered absolutely clearly her early days. She remembered the Irishman who fought every night with the Protestants outside the dirty noisy pub, and who returned with a black eye which he flaunted as if it were an honour brought back from an ancient unalterable war; she remembered the old coal cellar at the back and the padlock frosted on a winter morning: she remembered the children playing in front of the tenement in their dirty clothes: she remembered the bustle and movement, the drunken women shouting insults at each other, first taking the clothes' pegs out of their mouths: she remembered it all so clearly it was like an ache in her body.

"I was happy then," she thought, "I was never so happy as I was then and I didn't know it. I didn't know it at all." And the nostalgia flooded her so freshly that she almost cried with the pity of it. And Mrs Murphy too was part of that world, she recognised her as she might have recognised an old friend, she too might have walked up that stone stair to her room in that tenement, waddling and shouting, a brawling bow-legged Irishwoman. All those mornings so long ago, cold and clear, when one had been young, and busy. And now there was the becalmment . . .

"I'm sorry," she said to Mrs Murphy, "I didn't hear you."

36

"I was only saying that anytime you want to visit just come. Just walk up the stair and press the bell. I'm not like the people who . . . Do you know that there are some people now and they have this little thing on their door like an eye and they look through it and if they don't want to let someone in they pretend they're out. What's the world coming to? Tell me that."

And so Mrs Mallow sat there for over an hour and they talked about this and that but mostly about the past, and their thoughts and prejudices fitted each other, for they were both in a similar position, and their complaints and griefs and joys were of the same kind, and so they got on very well together, so that when Mrs Mallow finally and reluctantly left she felt as if she had found a friend whom she could trust, whom she could talk to, whose life to a certain extent duplicated her own : and the fact that Mrs Murphy was a Catholic didn't bother her at all, not in the slightest, though she wasn't very happy about the vulgarity of the green crib with the distorted donkeys or whatever they were : they offended her susceptibilities.

5

WHEN VERA HEARD about Mrs Murphy she felt more disturbed than she could rationally account for. Her disturbance was compounded of a number of factors. One was that Mrs Murphy was a Catholic. She hadn't thought that this would disturb her but it did. As had already been said her idea of the best kind of church was one of a chaste artistic almost mediaeval institution which no longer existed and probably never had. It was an aesthetic ideal rather than a religious one. But Mrs Murphy's Catholic church—or rather what she assumed it was— didn't fit her idea : it seemed to her to be vulgar, cheap and meretricious. She had somehow inherited, though not from her mother certainly, a concept of a church which had the rational moderation of the Protestant along with the mediaeval resonance of a more beautiful church. A church of nuns might have suited her, but she thought of the Catholic Church as not at all nun-like but aesthetic in a false way, in an unrigorous style. And this idea was reinforced by her mother's theatrical flirting with churches of a similar cheap nature : for example her mother had a brief but intense flush of enthusiasm for a Greek church whose proceedings were carried out entirely in a Greek language which she did not understand. Her mother loved grandiose ceremony, white clothes, singing, colour and pageantry, even the smell of incense. Even her clothes—a succession of streaming bizarre cloaks—were a manifestation of a religious plumage. And Vera had associated her mother with an emotional falsity which she had transferred to the church itself. Thus she felt a distaste which she would probably have admitted was irrational though nonetheless powerful.

At the same time she was disturbed that this woman—this Mrs Murphy—had been in the habit of cleaning stairs and belonged to a much lower class than herself. It was as if she represented a threat of some sort, the nature of which she did not fully understand, for she had not really known people like her in her own protected life. The closest she could get to her were the school cleaners whom she did not speak to, though she didn't deliberately choose not to. And the fact that the woman was Irish didn't help either. She had no knowledge of Ireland and she hadn't met any Irish people but she thought of them as opposed to order, difficult and too sociable. She did however like the poetry of Yeats which had more Protestant qualities.

She also felt a slight anger against her mother-in-law. Why had she complicated things in this way? Why couldn't she have struck up an acquaintance with a woman of her own class, some middle-class person from her own church, whom she would have more in common with. She should think of things like that: the fact that she hadn't showed a failure of tact and responsibility and, yes, even intelligence.

"I'm sure," she said to Tom, "that this woman, Mrs Murphy or whatever her name is, will want to visit her, or at least your mother will feel that she ought to ask her since after all she visited her."

"I don't see why," Tom replied, "and even if that were the case why shouldn't she come here? She wouldn't be in the house all the time."

They were lying in bed together, the window open, and a little light from the moon half dissipating the darkness.

"I just know that that will happen," Vera insisted. "It is in the nature of things."

Tom himself felt slightly confused, for he sensed Vera's disapproval, and he was bothered that the question had arisen, but now that it had he was determined to be fair.

"We can't after all say that she can't bring her here. We can't decide who her friends are to be."

He was worried about an incident that had happened in his class that day and which he had told Vera about. A girl had fainted, had keeled over in her seat, and he hadn't known what to do. It all happened very suddenly. She was a big girl and she lay there on the floor and a pool of water, which he later realised was urine, had formed about her.

He had stood there in a fixity of distaste mixed with panic, quite useless and remote. In fact another girl had taken charge. Later the school medical officer had come in and taken over and he had watched as the girl, her head between her knees, her hair falling downwards in a floating stream, had returned to consciousness. It was like seeing life transmit itself through a block of wood, for at first when the girl had been walked about the room she had looked as stiff as a log, but then it was as if a new dawn had arisen in a primitive world and the log had begun to feel the warmth of an early sun and come gradually alive. Expression had radiated from the log, and it was finally transformed to a human being again. It had worried him more that he could say to find that he had been totally helpless in front of that situation. Remembering the urine he had carefully avoided the girl's eye for the rest of the period.

"I know that," said Vera. "It's just that . . . it's difficult to explain. I'm not trying to be difficult about it. But it seems to me that in the first place these are not the kinds of people your mother should be with. I feel it in my bones."

"You don't understand," said Tom, "she's reverting to her early days, to the days when she was happiest. These are the kinds of people that she knew then. I can understand it. It's very simple."

"Simple? I should have thought that would have been the last word one would apply to it. You're being curiously opaque for once."

"I'm not being curiously opaque," Tom said with a slight flare of anger, "not at all. I'm trying to understand. In any case she can always take her to her room. We don't need to see her if we don't want to."

"Mm. That's easy to say. But what are the practical mechanics of it? I shall have to take tea in to them."

She did not feel that she wanted to be a maid to Mrs Murphy who after all had nothing to do with her : and in any case there was nothing of the servant in her nature.

"Well, I'll take it in then and I'll make it too if you like. In any case the situation hasn't arisen yet."

"That wouldn't look very nice," said Vera angrily. "It would be putting me in a false position."

"All right, then, you'll be put in a false position. But all this is surely very trivial. Aren't you making mountains out of molehills?"

"No I'm not and you know it," said Vera, sitting up in bed, her ghastly nightgown making her look momently like a nun.

40

"All these little things are very important. They are the ends of the wedge."

"What wedge?"

"Oh, nothing. If you can't see it you can't see it, and that's it."

There was a silence and in the silence Tom imagined his mother lying in bed in her own room, ignorant of what was being said about her.

"After all," he argued, "she's on her own and she needs someone. I don't see what all the fuss is about."

"All right, I won't mention it again till the situation arises and we'll just leave it there for the moment."

However, she thought that Tom was being unreasonable: he had this habit of calling important issues trivialities because he did not wish to face up to them. It came from that part of his nature which sometimes emerged in inane and unfunny jokes.

"In any case," said Tom, "your own mother had strange friends in the past. What about that Indian guru she brought to your house one night?"

"That was different. My mother was concerned with him intellectually. She . . ."

"Oh," Tom interrupted, "so long as it's intellectual it's OK, then. So long as she can say, 'I can bring any old tramp to my house, it's all part of the search for my identity'. He may be unshaven, stubbly, toothless and stink to high heaven but so long as he hides a piece of nirvana inside his dirty cloak and has a half-baked vision of the universe which involves astrology, spiritualism etc. he's all right. I call that snobbery."

"Call it what you like. It's a different situation, and even you must admit that."

"I don't admit it at all. I only see snobbery at the root of it."

There was another silence which this time prolonged itself. Vera had turned away from him, and Tom felt that she had done this as a tactical manœuvre.

"I'm damned if I'm going to talk," he told himself. "I'm damned if I'm going to say anything."

And he stared at the ceiling which glimmered with moonlight and thought about the girl who had fainted in his class, her wooden body, her doll-like perambulation about the room, her thaw and resurrection.

41

He thought to himself, "I am changing. Something is happening to me. Something strange is happening to me. I'm not sure that it is a good thing. I don't even know what it is."

Vera's face was turned away. In a sudden access of what might have been either affection or contrition he kissed her lightly on the cheek but he might have been kissing marble. She did not waken from what he knew was a pretended sleep.

Tom turned on his left side away from her, and so they slept back to back, he facing the open window, the draught from which slightly stirred the curtains.

Nevertheless something was happening to him, and it wasn't anything he could precisely focus on or name. It was as if in a late revelation he was coming into the Vale of Soul Making, as if across a flat autumn field he was seeing a strange slightly ominous structure rising, an airy web. His bringing his mother to his house was the result not the cause of this feeling. He had taken to thinking of her as totally alone, and he had found the thought unbearable. But he was perceptive enough to realise that his mother's loneliness—that perpetual image—was in a sense a displacement of his own loneliness, and when he saw her in his mind's eye as perhaps knitting by a window or pacing about an empty house it was himself he was seeing. Even after he had brought her to the house he thought of her as alone, and before he went to school in the morning he would shout "Cheerio" through the shut door, not knowing sometimes whether she was awake or asleep. He knew that she was trying to be as little bother as possible, but her attempts to diminish herself only paradoxically magnified her presence.

Sometimes the terrible thought came into his mind, "Vera is not really the sort of person who knows about my mother. She needs someone less rarefied, more, in a sense, vulgar and cheerful." But he did not blame Vera for being what she was. It was not easy for them to have their mother in the living room for after all they had preparation to do, and it would have been difficult for her to sit there in silence. Perhaps what they should have done was buy her a small house near themselves. But houses were expensive and scarce, and they almost certainly wouldn't have been able to get a suitable one in their immediate area

42

quite apart from the fact that paying a large mortgage they wouldn't have been able to afford one. And there was no reason to believe that she would have liked to live in a house by herself in a strange town, not at least till she had grown used to it and liked it.

He wondered if Vera had really wanted his mother there in the first place and whether now that she had heard about Mrs Murphy she might not turn against her. But what Vera didn't seem to realise was that though she herself had been used to loneliness and could exist on very little human contact his mother wasn't like that. She wasn't at all interested in books as Vera was, nor for that matter was she a devotee of television. She was in fact a very ordinary person without special gifts, without a high intelligence, though Tom was beginning to wonder about the value of intelligence even in his pupils. Surely it was more important to be "nice" than to be intelligent. In effect what world did *The Waste Land* reflect? For from day to day people lived in the world as it was, boring, dull, shot through with flashes of excitement and expectation, and at the end of it all a sort of white misty light as one might see sometimes between autumn trees.

One day he had a discussion about *King Lear* with his class, and it seemed to him that the play had taken on a new meaning for him, as if it were trying to teach him something. He found that for some odd reason his Sixth Year consisted almost exclusively of girls, which he didn't really mind, for though their minds lacked the penetration of those of boys—a certain ruthlessness—they compensated by a sensitivity that boys didn't have. They found *King Lear* not very interesting, which surprised him, but at least they had things to say about the king whom they considered little more than idiotic: nor did they condemn Goneril and Regan as much as he thought they might have done. No, there was no law inscribed on eternal tablets, which stated that one must look after the old, no matter what the latter were like. It all depended really on the individual old person. Certainly the bleak majesty of *King Lear* was very unlike the passive appeal of his own mother, and certainly the transformations and murders and wars belonged to a much earlier more barbaric world, but wasn't the principle timeless? No, they repeated, there existed no timeless decree by which we could all set our compass, no eternal moral north. And as he looked at them—young, pretty, earnest—he sometimes wondered what would happen to them, which ones would be stranded by the storms of life, and eventually live on the scraps of charity distributed by a family busy with their own concerns.

Even in the school itself he saw reflections of his own predicament. For instance there was a lady teacher who always brought her frail tottering ninety-year-old mother to all the school functions, looked after her with great affection, and in fact devoted her life to her, so that though she remained unmarried, she, in apparent joy, kept alive that old bundle of bones, but perhaps only so that she herself wouldn't be left alone. It was all very complicated.

Why should Vera object so strongly to that Irish woman? After all, she was an ordinary human being like his own mother.

6

ONE SUNDAY MORNING Tom made a momentous decision.
Casting his Sunday papers aside he announced that not only
would he take his mother to church but he would also attend
the service with her. Vera who had been standing at the cooker
turned and looked at him in amazement as if she had been struck
to the heart. Because his mother was already waiting to go, gloved
and coated, and carrying her bible in her hand, Vera didn't say
anything but he felt that he had somehow wounded her deeply,
and for the moment the pathos that surrounded his mother
transferred itself to his wife. Then Vera had turned away and
continued with her cooking in silence, and he had simply said
that they would be back at half past twelve.

"I shall expect you then," said Vera in an almost muffled
voice. At that moment she looked so defenceless and hurt that
he nearly went up to her and kissed her but her back, so elo-
quent of disapproval, discouraged him. He left the *Observer* and
the *Sunday Times* as a peace offering for her, unopened, unread.
At least, he thought, she should realise what an effort he was
making, in going against his own principles in the service of
another human being. She should surely thank him for taking
his mother off her hands for a whole morning. Surely that should
weigh in her judgment. His mother was waiting, trying not to
look pleased, as if she had sensed Vera's disapproval: but he
could tell nevertheless that his decision had made her happy.
What am I to do, he thought. I'm trying to be fair to both. It's
all very difficult. Human relationships are really impossible. One
tug here and there's an open wound there.

"Wouldn't you like to come yourself?" he asked Vera.

"No, you go," she said, in the same remote muffled voice. "I'll
have to do the cooking. You go. I don't really want to go."

And so they left. When they had gone Vera looked down
dully at the spoon in her hand. What was she expected to do?
Was she not doing her best? And now Tom was betraying his
own true self by going to church. As she stood there she remembered her mother, flamboyant and theatrical, setting off to her

church in Edinburgh, pulling on her red gloves in a flurry of excitement, as if there was a coach outside waiting. And she also remembered the compulsory church services she had had to attend when she was in school and which she had hated, as she had hated many of the pupils; their childish scurries in the dorm after lights out, the shared food parcels at midnight, the running into wardrobes and under beds when authority came to investigate. They had all been so infantile, their world was so uninteresting in comparison with that of for instance Jane Eyre. She remembered the stupid conspiracies with hot-water bottles and baths. And she suddenly felt overwhelmingly insecure as if someone were trying to disassemble her carefully structured world. Evil perhaps rose simply from that; fear, grief, absence, insecurity.

And now there was this new development which she couldn't help construing as a threat, Tom's going to church. What had happened to his, for want of a better word, integrity? How could one despise the empty robes and theatre of religion, how could one feel the utmost contempt for that bravado without substance, and then in such a short time and so inexplicably become a willing spectator of it, perhaps even an actor in it. It was true: she felt a new coldness about her, as if her formal world were in danger of destruction, a sentence which would soon lack a verb. In the chill of the autumn morning she left the kitchen and went to the bathroom and stood staring at the doll which was lying on the cistern facing her as she looked in. The eyes, blue and cloudless, gazed at her from below the long eyelashes. The face, round and chubby and red as an apple, showed an almost vulgar healthiness and absence of thought. The dress, short and frilled and golden, hardly reached the chubby knees.

Where had the doll come from? She couldn't remember. Had she got it as a marriage present? Surely not. Had she bought it in the town one day when she had nothing better to do? She couldn't remember at all. But there it stood on top of the cistern, mindless and clear-eyed confronting her head-achy untidy self, as if it were a symbol of a primitive time before religion had been even thought of, with its red lips, red ribbons and startlingly blue eyes which seemed to suggest a pagan heaven without mercy or fear. She picked it up in her hand, weighing

46

it delicately, and then began to stroke the golden hair very gently and tenderly as if she were stroking the head of a child, over and over, a stiff staring child golden in the autumnal light.

7

MEANWHILE TOM SAT beside his mother in the church after a moment of hesitation at the door, as if even then he could turn back and not commit himself. He saw a number of people whom he knew and who nodded at him in slight surprise, glancing at his mother who smiled in an almost queenly manner. As he waited for the service to begin, looking around him at the bright hats of the women, the tall blue cross on the pulpit cloth, the varnished pulpit with the microphone, the narrow windows with their stained-glass panes, he thought of what he was doing. His mother sat beside him, staring straight ahead of her, her hands in her lap, passive in the silence, and he sensed that in some way she was repossessing him, that by doing what he had done he had taken an irrevocable step. For what he was doing, and his motive for doing it, was unusual. Not believing in religion, he had placed humanity above ideology as if by doing so he was setting himself beside her in the world, as if he was showing that he was not ashamed of her.

This extraordinary achievement—the clearsightedness with which he had seen the issues at stake—warmed him with a righteous glow. How many people would have understood what he had understood, that beyond ideology, that even beyond disbelief, there lies the human being, solitary and vulnerable: that more important than intellectual consistency is the helpless demand of the human soul and body: that from these stale forms peers out shyly and timidly the human face, lost in a world that it does not understand. How easy really it had all been, and how few understood how much it had cost him to sit where he was now sitting. And yet if one did not believe in religion was it any worse than going to a performance in a theatre, a willing surrender of disbelief? Or, if one considered the whole thing as a routine act, like having a weekly injection, why could one not bear it with a smile?

It seemed to him that when the minister entered, dignified in his black robes and carrying a bible in his hand, he was paying special attention to him, as if he were a hero who had done something magnificent and unique: and when he preached his sermon which was about the Parable of the Talents he felt that it was he himself, talented and sensitive, who was being referred to.

When the psalms were sung, he found himself back again in the world of his childhood, a word of settled order, which on the whole it had been. Nor was it the psalms alone that recalled that world. It was also the smell of varnish from the seats, the slight coughs of members of the congregation, the colour of the psalm books themselves. He thought of the world of the Bible as a secure aesthetic world, with shepherds watching their sheep on patches of sunny green, boats floating in water, stars shining in the sky, staffs and beards, skies of eternal blue above brown deserts. Yet at the same time he did not believe that this world represented any form of immortality, nor was the church itself anything other than a building of stone built by mortal hands. Nor did he believe that anyone had ever risen from the dead, nor in miraculous interventions. None of these was a truth to him, they were simply beautiful images, poetic and colourful, a vanished primitive world.

But he believed that his mother rested secure in that world. Her faith was simple, though it seemed to have little to do with her daily living. For instance at that moment she might be thinking, for all he knew, that she had won some sort of triumph over Vera, and this triumph perhaps was making her singing sweeter. Life was terrible, it was a truly terrible thing, and its issues beyond our understanding, for deeper even than religion was the terror and glory of the human mind. How could one live at all with people? How did people ever manage to live together, tugging and pulling, shouting silently, "I am, I am, listen to me, I am here. Pay attention to me. Love me without return, gratuitously, with utter constancy."

When the service was over he walked among the congregation, was shaken hands with by the minister who recognised him (for he had a daughter in the school) and whose smile was as benignant as the sun. He introduced his mother to a friend of his who taught at the school and was an elder of the church, and in the after-service bustle felt about him a warmth which might have been false and meretricious, but was welcome just the same. It was clear to him that his mother was happy to be at his side: after all he was her son and he had a recognised place in the community. The desert was blossoming like the rose, he was showing charity and kindness, he was being what he ought to be, a man who loved his mother and who showed it before the world. He was successful in his own small way.

Side by side they walked to the car, their shoes rustling the gravel, while near them lay the graveyard with its tombs ordered and clean in the morning light. He could see flowers here and there, vases, open stone bibles, the glitter of granite from the gravestones, he could even hear a late autumnal bird twittering from the churchyard. How silent and pure that world was, the world of the dead, with its iron railings and mostly ancient stone. How clearly it told in its very dumbness of the continuity of life even in death, of ancestries that perpetuated themselves through centuries, for to this place the living came with their flowers and in turn others would bring bouquets to them. How well the world was organised, and how simple life really was. How little the intellect had to do with it. There were only a few clear necessary truths which one could carry with one as if in an overnight bag with its toothbrush and shaving gear. The rest could be left to itself. He opened the door of the car for his mother and she got in, arranging her coat. Then she sat back in the car, her bible in her lap, looking relaxed and at peace, heading for home.

8

ONE MORNING VERA woke up feeling very cheerful, Tom still lying in bed gazing at the ceiling. An idea had blossomed in her mind during the night and stood there clearly before her, as if it had emerged without her intervention or presence at all. It was a fine beautiful creative idea of the kind that visits one perhaps on a summer morning when the sun is shining and the curtains shake a little in the breeze: but this one had blossomed on an autumn day.

"You're very happy this morning," said Tom lazily.

"Not particularly," Vera replied carelessly for as yet she did not wish to tell him of her idea which she hugged to herself as if it were a child loved secretly for itself alone. She combed her hair in the mirror while Tom watched her. If only she were a nun, fulfilled in the world of her cool vocation: but that was not possible. Nowadays one must live in the world and the world made demands which had to be met: it required that one get up in the morning, set out into its infinitely devious maze, meet with other people and have relations with them, useful or futile.

Even from our loved ones, she thought, we hide most of our secret wishes and dreams. For instance at this moment Tom does not know what I'm thinking and I don't know what he's thinking. Nevertheless we are able to live together as if we knew each other wholly, which is an impossibility: for how could she have known that Tom would have surrendered the convictions of a lifetime in order to go to church? Nor had he even talked about what had happened when he came home, and when she had questioned him he had given unsatisfactory and vague answers as if this was a part of his life that he did not wish to talk about to her, or as if it was simply impossible for him to talk about it. He would have considered her interest trivial not realising how important his action had been to her. It was as if their marriage were beginning to cloud slightly like a window on an autumn or winter morning when it is enwrought with cold patterns of ice so that one cannot see through it as one could when the weather was warm and unclouded and sunny. Exactly like the bedroom window on that very morning so that she could not see the trees in their autumn bravery until she rubbed it with her hand.

"Should you not be getting up?" she asked.

"In a minute," said Tom, lying there in the warmth of the bed.

She shook her hair back, put on her clothes and went to the bathroom while he still lay there. What am I? he wondered. Who am I? What is the meaning of my life? Why am I going to school this morning? Why is that wardrobe with the mirror standing in front of me at this particular moment? Why is her hairbrush with strands of her hair in it lying on the dressing table? And he gazed at it as if it were an object that he had never seen before, dear and distant, the pink hairbrush which contained part of his wife's body. And the conjunction of the hairbrush and her hair and the dressing table puzzled him so that he found it difficult to imagine why they had come together in that room, like spaceships emerging from the depths of an unknown universe.

He suddenly threw back the bedclothes from him and looked at himself in the mirror. His long narrow face gazed back at him, his eyes examined his reflected eyes, his nose thrust itself forward, his mouth with the prim pursed lips was reflected back at him. He pushed his face against the glass as if against an icy window and burst out into a manic laugh as if he wished to explode in front of the mirror, as if he wished both reality and reflection to merge with each other in the infinite depths of the glass. Then he began to dance in his shirt in front of the mirror, moving his body backwards and forwards in a parody of Top of the Pops and as he did so he was laughing helplessly and silently while his distorted waltzing image gazed back at him.

After he had done this for some time he put on his trousers and when his wife returned from the bathroom he went and busied himself with the tedious business of shaving. While he was doing so, his wife in her turn was sitting on the bed, gazing into the mirror and examining her face as if to assure herself that she had lost none of that quality, whatever it was, that had first attracted Tom. She was wondering if she ought to do her hair in a different way, or perhaps wear make-up which she ordinarily never did. I didn't know I was like this, she thought with surprise, I didn't think that I was like an animal scenting trouble from a distance, sensing some other as yet unfocussed predator moving stealthily towards it. She was amazed that these thoughts had come to her since she was not at all imaginative but as she sat there she wondered what it would be like for an animal to feel itself being stalked, death steadily nearing in the long grass. But she was not so helpless as a small animal might be: she could do something about what was happening. She was not going to wait till the teeth bit into her. She was going to do something about it.

And she briskly made the bed with obsessive tidiness. She put the brush away in the drawer removing as much of the hair as she could and placing it in a small coloured bucket that stood in one corner of the room. She turned at the door to make sure that everything was neat and in its proper place before leaving and then she went and made the breakfast.

The two of them, she and Tom, were silent at breakfast as they usually were for Tom was not the sort of person who was conversational in the early morning, nor for that matter was she. A part of her mind was already thinking about her classes and how she would present a particular lesson. She was thinking that she might try to get another cupboard for her room, or a new blackboard of the sort that rolled round and round. Even in the car—whose windows were almost frosted over—they were silent, Tom driving with his usual negligent speed, both of them gazing out of small spaces between the frost at the uniformed pupils who were walking up the road. There they were, willing or unwilling to be educated, and there were the two of them responsible for their education. What a privilege, she thought, what a life's work. What an immensely complicated thing, he was thinking, what an intricate and often useless business.

The car drew up outside the school and he kissed her briefly before they set off for their respective rooms. As yet there was no one in her room and she stood at the table looking around her at the empty desks, briefly glancing at the blackboard, allowing the day to ascend steadily in her so that she would be able to meet it with whatever knowledge and readiness that she had. She looked at the posters on the walls and felt that she was in her proper place in life, the place that she would probably occupy till she retired. This was her life's work and she was good at it, she was in control of it. Here the unreasonable was converted into the reasonable, and the inarticulate made articulate. She was a colonist of partially unknown minds, a missionary assimilating new areas to literacy. She waited happily for the class to enter and had almost forgotten her mother-in-law and Tom in the excitement of anticipation and conversion, as if she were a secular nun married to her work. Sometime she would have to try some drama with them, perhaps a little play about an old woman. She knew exactly which girl she would choose to play the part. She had tried drama before but hadn't done it very well. But she thought that the next time she tried it she might do it competently and with imagination.

Meanwhile in another room Tom was sitting alone, at his desk, waiting. Round him too the school gathered and he assumed the day like a cloak (though in fact he never wore one: his wife, however, always did). Through the window he could see the rowan tree still partially in blossom, its red berries bright as drops of blood, its branches airy and light. The sun made a straight line across the floor to his desk, direct as a ruler. Through the open door he could see the pupils standing at a radiator with newspapers in their hands as they studied the football results. The hall was being prepared for the morning service with seats already laid out. "Oh Christ," he thought, "here we go again." The school itself was like a church, ancient, finished, and again with the bubble of laughter that sometimes arose in him spontaneously he thought, "Down that street man must go, bearing only his honour, believing in nothing, a corrupt knight in a corrupt society. Through the Waste Land a man must go, through Margate, feet outstretched on a canoe. "Nothing, nothing, do you hear nothing?" "Nothing will come of nothing. Speak again." "What is that voice under the door?"

And yet . . . And yet . . . The children were not wholly corrupt. They came like seagulls, their beaks outstretched for food. I love them, he thought, I do not love the institution, I love the children. It is they who in their freshness must save the world, though the old must be saved too. It is the human being who must be saved, not this building of stone. If the freshness could only be retained, if the fresh voices would speak and sing, if the unpredictable could survive. Love is all we have. But how hellishly difficulty it was to

54

share out our love to everyone, when so many beaks were thrust at one.

Those children, ready to set out into the world with hope in their eyes, how much he loved them. He himself must once have been like them, unclouded and clear. How beautiful they were, how fresh, how lovable. What a privilege it was to have them in his room, to be in a sense responsible for them. What a grave responsibility it was to feed their minds. What a glory among all the terror. His mother too must have been like them once, though perhaps not so intelligent, hopefully setting out into the future, careless of what it might bring. And look what it had actually brought her.

The bell rang and here they were sitting in front of him. Waiting. For their minister. For the food of the day. And as he started reading *The Waste Land* he could hear from the hall the uninspired singing of 'To Be a Pilgrim'.

9

AT ELEVEN O'CLOCK the bell rang and the teachers went to the school dining room for their coffee. There they sat at tables, joked, complained. They discussed children, the unfairness of time-tables, the difficulty of certain classes, the administration which ensured that they did not hear of anything till it was too late. Bearded men mixed with clean-shaven ones, oldish women with very definite views on education mixed with the eager young who were still enthusiastically experimenting. The hubbub was as loud as in any class that had been left unattended. And to the dining room Vera came with the others, though she did not like being among so many people. However she did not want to miss anything of importance, any gossip, any major or minor step that was being taken.

It was a world of people brought together by their daily work, making concessions here and there in the service of others. It was a world of tedium and a world of interest. To it willingly or unwillingly each came with his or her own burden of the day. There was Mr Dawson who complained about everything, whose response to all initiatives was a mechanical "No", and who, him-self lazy and uncooperative, would complain endlessly about lazy and uncooperative pupils. There was Miss Glenn, fresh-faced, efficient and future-loving, who had never in her short life had any doubts about her vocation, and who had dedicated herself utterly to her work till the day when she would receive her token of esteem and step out into the universe without bells or altering children; and Mr Leitch, abrupt and almost brutal, who taught with insensitive conviction and who might equally well have been a farmer or a salesman.

There was the shy Miss Bryce who found great difficulty in controlling her classes, and whose dedication was therefore greater than that of most of the others, for her conscience would not let her alone, and lay beside her even in her bed at night, issuing in terrible dreams of upset chairs and great wild laughing faces. There was Mr Grieve who, once an artist, had found his final happiness in teaching others how to draw and paint, whose room was a celebration of his contentment, and who believed sincerely that one day, yes, one day, he would discover an artist of immense natural talent who might in his interview on TV mention his name as the man who had influenced him most.

It was in fact a whole world that gathered in the dining room. And each moved away from or towards the others in a dance of mutual attraction or repulsion. Sometimes one would find oneself with one group and then another as interests or activities changed. A certain bluffness discouraged melancholy, curiosity encouraged gossip. The school had in some vast random manner gathered all these people together and set up relationships within it. Some loved it, some hated it, some tolerated it, some complained about it. But outside the school there lay another world, considered physically and metaphysically, which became more and more distant, and was often feared. The school itself was an affair of bells and rooms. Into it year after year came the children and then the children, almost unnoticeably, changed and left. Their faces duplicated those of their parents. It was a vast family, boisterous and protected. It was a womb and a museum and a place of learning. Scarred desks told of those who had been there and left.

Inside that world as in any other world people complained and were inconsistent. They wished to be elsewhere at times but there was nowhere else to go. They were frightened at times, happy at other times. A single achievement would make them feel like gods, a single failure would dishearten them. The seasons flowered and withered, and these were dominated by the tasks of the year. It was seldom that any major disaster happened, but minor accidents were magnified. One need not be lonely in the school for if one surrendered to it one could find fulfilment. One could shine with its poor glory, one could live inside one's dream. One could demand that uniforms should be made compulsory, or one could not. Each could be himself within limits, and those limits were created by the continual rubbing against others, whose personalities were different and therefore sacred.

The school could be considered as a theatre or a church, a continually changing scene or one dominated by rules. It could be dignified or flamboyant but never silent. It was a world which reflected the outer world and as such it had to be borne, for the alternative was worse, the alternative was another world of still greater silence or greater noise, of diminished humanity or loss. And yet if one had come in and looked and listened to it, it would have seemed noisy and cheerful, with people talking intently to others, drinking coffee, smoking cigarettes, holding brief conferences while standing up, cups in hands.

Miss Donaldson sat among the others, though curiously separate from them at one of the tables, smoking heavily as she always did. It was one of the school jokes that someone who taught R.E. (Religious Education) should find it necessary to smoke more than the acknowledged agnostics and atheists. Perhaps, they surmised, she also drank, in secret. Not that anyone knew very much about her, except that she had not been very long at the school, that she had taken over the R.E. classes because no one else was willing to do so, and that she didn't seem particularly happy. Certainly she wasn't a great talker. But the others were content to have her since otherwise it would have meant that they would have to take some of the R.E. classes themselves. R.E. was not taken seriously: indeed all it really meant was that classes were sent to a particular room where it was assumed, sometimes wrongly, that they would be given some instruction on the bible. But in fact no one knew whether they were being taught about religion or not.

Miss Donaldson was a very odd sort of person with a white slab of a face, a stout body, and very large feet: she walked in a limping manner often imitated by her pupils. She had taken a philosophy degree, had taught in other more difficult schools in the city, and had finally found herself at this particular one. She hated what she was doing, for most of the pupils came to her, determined not to work, and would prevent her from doing anything by asking her questions which would set her off, against her better inclinations, down strange tracks of Hinduism, drug addiction, alcoholism and sometimes even sexual mania.

"What about Hell then, miss?" they would ask her. "Do you believe in Hell then, in the tortures and that?" Or, "Do you believe Jesus rose from the dead, miss?" Or, "What did Jesus look like miss? Was he yellow or what?" And then disorganised arguments would start, someone implying that he was a Paki, others imitating Pakistani accents, saying, "Thank you very much, miss.

I am thanking you a great deal, miss." Sometimes they would say, "Why do we have to do R.E., miss? Why do we have to do it if we don't believe in it? Do you believe in it, miss?" "Tell us about the Catholics, miss. Is it true that the Pope is infallible?" And one or two of the older and more daring pupils would wave green and white scarves shouting, "Cel-tic, Cel-tic." "Is it true that the Catholics worship idols, miss? It says in the Bible not to worship the Golden Calf, isn't that right, miss?" "What's the Golden Calf then," someone would ask as if attracted by some divine rustic vision, glimpsed perhaps momently on the farm from which he came and where he would look after the cattle during week-ends.

Philosophy never taught me this, she would think cynically, philosophy taught me that there was a calmer world than this where bearded tranquil men would speculate about matter, forms, language, morality, with an ease and luxury divorced from the concerns of everyday.

"Do you believe God has a beard, miss?" "Twit, do you think he's got a stash then?" "What about the Pope, miss? Why doesn't the Pope ever get married." Then there would be a communal whisper from which she would hear as if floating on another air the single word "Balls" and she would feel a primitive desire sometimes so intolerably strong that it would nearly overwhelm her.

No, truly this was not what philosophy had taught her. In those university days when she was studying Philosophy she had lived in an exalted fever of study, in an atmosphere of libraries, imagining that the "real world" was that of Kant, whose mind worked like a watch, or that of Wittgenstein whose personality attracted her so much that she thought she was in love with him. It seemed to her that his idea of a one-to-one relationship of objects with the parts of the speech of the language was a beautiful concept which made reality meaningful and radiant. But now here she was teaching R.E. to pupils who did not want to listen.

How had it all happened? Well first of all she found that there was little she could do with her philosophy degree except teach. When she was in university she had never thought of what she would do with her life afterwards: that would have been too vulgar, too empirical: that would have been the sort of instrumentalism that derived from Dewey. Thus when naked she had arrived at last in the winds of reality she was like a bird whose feathers shake in the bad weather. And she had found herself in a school in Glasgow whose doors had never been darkened or lightened by any knowledge of Hegel, and whose roughness almost destroyed her.

She would not have stayed long in that school if her mother had not been alive in those days. It was she who had kept her there, nailed her to the classroom so that she felt as if she was being slowly crucified. Many a time she would have walked out of the doors forever, anywhere at all, without destination, if it hadn't been for her mother who would say to her,

"But what will I do? I have no money. What am I going to live on?" And she would add,

"I brought you up. I sent you to university. You owe me something or don't you think you do?"

And her conscience, sterile and bitter, had allowed that this was the case. Sometimes she would walk for hours on the streets at night, among the flaring yellow lights, as if looking for some deliverer among these lamps that bowed down like aged scholars casting their small pale halos on the stone. But she had found none, or at least not a permanent one. Once she had got gloriously drunk and had shouted at her mother as if the latter were a warder keeping her in prison with the iron key of filial gratitude.

In that school she had found one person with whom she had gone out once or twice. He was a middle-aged man who taught music and who gave her, once, a box of chocolates addressed to "Ma cherie". His primness and affectedness would often make her laugh when she was away from him, and she certainly didn't love him, but she would have been willing to marry him in order to get out of her nightmare. But she realised eventually that he would never marry, his selfishness was too firmly embedded. Unlike her he was reasonably happy where he was—his dramatic flourish of the baton at annual school concerts satisfied him. Even his taste for music—his hero was Tchaikovsky—seemed to her to be suited to him, a vulgar dream of heroic narrative. One night he promised to meet her at a concert but she hadn't gone, partly because her mother had felt pains about her heart, and when she had met him on the following day he had turned away. He was, she concluded, incapable of loving her, of loving anyone. Men were childish careless creatures of the moment, their boxes of chocolates meaningless gifts. Nevertheless she often felt unsatisfied physical desires which tormented her: and these she found affected the clarity of her mind, and became an instrument of torture like a very fine needle.

One day her mother had died—she had had after all a bad heart, it wasn't just a phantom of her imagination—and when she had tidied up all the family affairs, being the only offspring and her father no longer alive, she had left the school she was in and had made a leap towards this one, for by that time she was thirty-eight years old, and there was nothing else that she could do. They had been happy to have her, for the classes had been without an R.E. teacher for a year: they would have been happy to have anyone, she later realised.

She stayed by herself in a small flat in the centre of the town and to this flat she returned night after night and spent the weekends there as well for she had nowhere else to go. Sometimes at nights as she read or watched TV, for she did no preparation for her school work after the first six months, she felt herself being shaken as if by physical waves of aggression, and at nights she was convulsed by sexual dreams in which she was the main protagonist. Limbs and eyes and breasts surged around her as in a Picasso painting, she found herself in tunnels where trains crowded with naked bodies rushed straight at her, seeking her, and aboard the trains were schoolboys shouting "Why did you never marry, miss? Was Jesus a poof, miss?"

It was not that she wasn't interested in religion, in fact she no longer believed in it. She had found herself in a situation that she couldn't get out of, so that her solution was simply to teach the Bible as if it were any other historical book. But the children perhaps sensing this—"the buggers know everything" she would say to anyone who cared to listen—kept at her, forcing her to explore the trivialities of the human, and not the divine, probing her weaknesses.

61

"I sometimes think I am evil," she would say to herself. "I really think I am evil." And at times evil would attract her not simply as a concept but as a living thing. She felt that she could have been a witch, that she could have celebrated a Black Mass, that she could have hung the cross upside down, read from a book consecrated to the devil, sung hymns and psalms backwards in a blasphemous gibberish.

Other times however she would rise on a sunny morning as if there was some destination still left to her, as if she could set off on a train somewhere to another place far from where she was, as if she could carelessly thumb a lift into a distant future. But as the day passed and the sun declined she knew that she was where she was, fixed and hopeless, and that she would probably be there forever.

How had it all happened? How had the trains of Plato and the rest sped off into another universe leaving her standing among rusting rails where small discontented shabby men held up their dirty green trivial flags? How had the roughness of reality come upon her so suddenly?

But it was the sexual nightmares that made life almost unbearable. It was these that had dulled her mind, that left her restless and unsatisfied, as, thick and heavy and limping as a frog, a demon frog on fire, she made her way through the world. She was like a frog on fire, turning back, quivering in the flame, its limbs spread out, a blackened evil star.

"Miss, did Jesus pee like anyone else?"

"If he was a god how could he pee, twit?"

"I was only asking."

"Shove off."

"Miss, what was the cross like? How big were the nails? Did they have nails like we have? Did they hammer them in, miss?"

Oh the terrifying multiplicity of the world, its trivial inanity. Theologians never told you about the length of the nails, the feelings of the alien people, the kinds of fishing boats they used, the taste of the wine they drank, the sorts of fish they ate. And yet these were the questions that her pupils were always asking, the irrelevant questions that had nothing to do with the tranquilities of theology. Nothing at all to do with the mind, only with the body, its sordid functions, its idiotic appearances. She raised her head from the table where the rings left by the coffee cups intersected with each other and stared straight at Vera Mallow.

10

MRS MALLOW AND Mrs Murphy had got into the habit of going for tea together in the morning and then taking a walk around the town. Sometimes they would sit on a bench by the sea and look out across the water, at the bare green island opposite. Mrs Mallow found the place more beautiful, more relaxing, than she had expected and in a strange way she was happy, though certain things worried her. Vera worried her, as she found it very difficult to speak to her, and there was a certain glacial air about her daughter-in-law which bothered her. In spite of that she felt more secure in the town than she had felt in Edinburgh, though there was one incident which when she looked back on it made her wonder if she really felt as happy as she should have. One afternoon she had gone to the railway station and had sat there staring at the trains, as if she wished to be setting out on one. It was an odd sensation, watching these trains, the flag men, the porters, as if at any time she expected to see her husband again walking towards her through a cloud of steam and inviting her to go with him to wherever he was going, so that for a moment she felt light-hearted, and was almost ready to step forward from her bench to be with him. But that had only happened one afternoon. Still it had been slightly disturbing.

But otherwise she felt more cheerful than she had expected, especially as she had found a friend she could talk to.

"There's one thing anyway," Mrs Murphy would say, "when you're like me you can do anything you like. You can go anywhere you like. I can get up tomorrow morning and go to Ireland if I feel like it. Not that I want to go. But I can. How are you getting on up there yourself?"

She talked of "up there" as if she had assigned Mrs Mallow's son and daughter-in-law to the "hill" where lived all those people who belonged to Rotary Clubs, Inner Wheels and posh houses.

"All right," said Mrs Mallow, "I'm getting on fine."

"Are you sure?"

"Yes, I'm sure."

"Oh well if you're sure you're sure, I didn't get on with my daughter-in-law at all. There were little things you see." And she would suddenly look out into the distance and say "The steamer's late today. Usually it's ten o'clock. What time do you make it? It's half an hour late. Anyway as I was saying, I didn't get on with her at all. She would get on my nerves. She would sit in front of me when I was watching the TV in her house. Her chair was next to the TV, you see, and she would sit there and I would say, 'I can't see the TV for you,' and she would shift over a bit, but after that she would be back again in the same place. She was doing it, trying it on, the same miss. After a while I never watched the TV at all. She was trying it on the wrong lady." And she squared her shoulders and looked at Mrs Mallow with suddenly fierce eyes, "I wasn't going to take her snash. Anyway I was paying for my own groceries. Don't you take any snash from anybody. Are you paying?"

"I offered to pay," said Mrs Mallow, "but they didn't want anything."

"You should have paid them," Mrs Murphy pronounced, nodding her head vigorously. "You should have paid them. If you pay they can't say anything to you. If I was you I'd pay."

"Would you?" Mrs Mallow asked meekly.

"I would," Mrs Murphy repeated emphatically. "I would. They wouldn't have anything to cast up at me. My mother taught me that. 'Always pay your way' she would say to me. My mother was a big woman and she brought up seven of us. 'You pay,' she would always say, 'hold your head up high.' My husband, though, he was different. He drank a bit. He worked on the roads and he drank. One night I threw him out but he was back the next day: you know, he had slept in the railway station that night. He used to joke and laugh all the time, you couldn't be angry with him for long, he had all the charm of the Irish as they say. He died ten years ago: he was very brave, a very brave man. Sometimes in the mornings I can still see him at the basin splashing water all over himself for he was very clean, I give him that. He came from Connemara. We used to fight all the time and then he would come home from his work and tell me to put on good clothes and we would go out to a hotel and he would splash out.

He was a very kind man. But he used to drink a hell of a lot," and she laughed, remembering him tenderly.

"You know," she said, "you've nothing to be ashamed of. After all you brought him up. Why shouldn't he look after you in your old age? That's what I'd like to know. Though, mind you, I didn't look after my own mother. I left her to marry Sean. Even then he used to drink but I never thought anything of it. 'You'll rue the day,' my mother used to say to me, but I didn't care. When we're young we don't listen to anybody. And I left her. She died when I was over here. I didn't stay to look after her, but people have their own lives to live, have they not, that's what I always say. You can't be looking after people all the time. Don't let them bother you."

A beautiful haze lay over the water, and through it Mrs Mallow could see two elegant grey ships side by side as if they had landed there like birds. In front of them, in a clearer space, a number of seagulls were squabbling in a ring for pieces of bread which were floating in the sea. Now and again one of them would rise from the quarrelling circle only to be pursued by another one, trying to make it drop the bread which it held in its beak.

The thought suddenly came into her head. "Maybe it would be better for me to live with Mrs Murphy. Wouldn't that be a good idea?" But she knew that that wouldn't happen, for in spite of her friendship with Mrs Murphy, she knew that she couldn't live with her. Mrs Murphy didn't have a good flat and as one got older one liked one's comforts. Tenements were all right in one's youth, but not in age.

"I'll tell you what," said Mrs Murphy, "why don't we go and have a look at the castle? How would you like to take a walk there? It's not far. Can you manage that?"

"Yes, I would like that," said Mrs Mallow though she would have preferred to stay where she was, gazing into the blue haze ahead of her.

"Come on then," said Mrs Murphy decisively, rising to her feet and setting off in her brisk duck-like walk, nodding now and again to people whom she knew and at one point saying, "That's an old bitch that one. You wouldn't think it to look at her, but she's going with another man. And she's an ugly old bitch right enough."

They left the road and climbed a brae to the castle, Mrs
Murphy heading upwards at a strong pace, and Mrs Mallow
following more slowly and carefully behind.

"I don't know much about this castle," Mrs Murphy said,
"there's no roof on it for a start. It used to be owned by a duke,
I think. These old buggers lived off the poor, you know. Every
one of them." After climbing for a little while they arrived at
the remains of a castle, roofless, doorless and with broken walls.
They stood on the hollow grassy floor and gazed downward over
the sea, while all around them there was a sudden twittering of
disturbed birds.

"He would have lived here, this duke, in the old days," said
Mrs Murphy, "but he went the way of the rest of them. Six
feet of earth like everybody else."

"The sea looks beautiful from here," said Mrs Mallow drawing
back a little from the wall as she gazed outwards. Ahead of
her she could see islands bluish in the haze and behind them
towering hills. She was still gasping a little after the climb.

She thought that it would have been splendid to have lived in
that castle when it had been in good condition; it had such a
commanding view across the straits, though now it was inhabited
only by birds, and littered with empty beer bottles. The breeze
from the sea blew in her hair and freshened her face so that
she felt suddenly young and strong again.

"That's where I stay," said Mrs Murphy pointing.

"Where do I stay?" Mrs Mallow asked.

"Over there. On that hill. Can you see it?"

"Yes, I can see it," said Mrs Mallow, realising that from this
height and distance the house looked small and unimportant. It
was just another house among many, not specially large or
impressive.

Mrs Murphy was staring down at what appeared to be the
remains of a bra. "Disgusting," she said, and then,

"They say that that Duke was connected with the Queen and
used to attend her at the Coronation."

In the distance Mrs Mallow could see the smoke rising from
chimneys, and a train winding like a green snake through the
hills, sunlight sparkling from its windows. It was as if her
troubles, her niggling worries, had all gone, and she could see

them like tiny houses diminished on that clear dry autumn day, which framed the scene below her like a picture hung in a railway carriage.

"There's a lot of shit here," said Mrs Murphy irritably, looking down at her shoes and rubbing them vigorously against the green wet grass. "That's the one thing you get among these old castles."

And Mrs Mallow burst out laughing and she couldn't stop. Mrs Murphy gazed at her in amazement, and she started to laugh too, and suddenly the two of them, like two maniacs in a roofless house, swayed together, laughing, Mrs Mallow's laughter being increased by her friend's comic splay-legged appearance, against that magnificent landscape, and Mrs Murphy's equally increased by the sight of this normally quiet woman in her brown coat convulsed and rocking backwards and forwards, sometimes having to steady herself by placing one hand on the broken wall in front of her. Eventually they stopped and wiped their eyes; Mrs Murphy made another fierce effort to clean her shoes: and then they walked down the brae to the promenade.

11

"WHAT EXACTLY ARE you trying to do?" said Tom to Vera, "inviting that bloody woman to the house. You know she's practically crazy. None of the pupils like her. What put it into your head anyway?"

"I was going to do a project on Joseph and his brothers," said Vera, "and I thought she might be able to give me some ideas, some books."

"But surely you didn't have to invite her to the house. For dinner. I don't understand you. You never invited people before. And she's such an old bag."

Very put down her sewing and said quietly but firmly, "I don't, as you say, invite many people to the house but I thought, among other things, that she might meet your mother." Her eyes gazed blandly at him, blue as a doll's.

"My mother!"

"Well, why not? She doesn't meet anybody apart from that Mrs Murphy. She might have something in common with Ruth Donaldson. After all she's quite religious. In fact . . ."

"In fact what?"

"I thought we might invite Mrs Murphy as well."

Tom stared at her in astonishment. What on earth was she up to? Mrs Murphy, his mother and Ruth Donaldson.

"After all," Vera continued calmly, "it's you yourself who were saying that I was an elitist and that I was only interested in intellectuals. I'm sure your mother and Mrs Murphy would be quite happy to have dinner with Ruth Donaldson. She's not a monster, you know. She's just a lonely person."

Tom, who felt that he had been outmanoeuvred but wasn't exactly sure how or why he should have been, said, "It worries me when I don't understand what you're up to. Why couldn't you just have invited Mrs Murphy to meet my mother? Why that woman?"

"I told you. She's lonely. She might have something in common with the two of them. I believe that she herself looked after her mother for a while."

"I didn't know that," said Tom. "And how exactly did you find that out? I thought she hardly spoke to anyone."

"Well, she spoke to me. She was quite talkative in fact. All she was wanting was someone to talk to. She is very pleased to have been asked. I don't think she's been out for ages."

"I can believe that," said Tom viciously. "And am I supposed to attend the dinner as well?"

"Naturally you're invited," And Vera smiled coolly.

"I see."

Quite without thinking Tom looked up at the pictures on the walls and said, "I'm beginning to get fed up with Hockney. Why don't we get some other people for a change? Some of the Dutch painters, for instance."

"If you like," Vera conceded, still sewing.

"Right then. We'll do that."

After a pause during which Vera's head was still bent over her embroidery, he said, "It was nice of Mr and Mrs Stewart to write to my mother and say how much they liked the house."

"Yes, wasn't it?"

"It's a child of six they have, isn't it?"

"I think so. I think that's what they said."

"I wonder why they're not buying their own home. Why they're renting one."

"Perhaps they can't afford one at the moment."

"Perhaps. But he seems to have a good job."

"I had gathered he was an accountant, yes."

"Maybe they're saving up. And after all they are getting the house very reasonably."

"Yes."

There was another longer pause before Tom spoke again :

"My mother seems to have taken a liking to TV all of a sudden."

"I think she doesn't want to come into the room while we're working. It's nothing more than that."

"Perhaps you're right. That bloody R.E. woman."

"What did you say?"

"Nothing. I only said that I don't like that R.E. woman. Still, now that you've invited her we can't very well say that she can't come."

70

"It would certainly be awkward."

"I understand," Tom continued relentlessly, "that she didn't talk much to the women in the staffroom. How did you get so friendly with her all of a sudden?"

"I felt sorry for her, and I talked to her at coffee. And, as I said, I want to do this project. There is no deep plot, you know." She raised her eyes and looked directly into his. "There isn't," she repeated. "Any more than there was when you took your mother to church."

"What did you say?"

"Nothing particular. I don't think there was any deep plot in your taking your mother to church."

"Why should the thought have entered your mind in the first place?"

"I've just been telling you that I don't think there was."

"Semantics," said Tom vigorously. "What have the two things to do with each other?"

"Nothing. Did I say that they had anything to do with each other? I said that in neither case was there any evidence of any deep plot. They were spontaneous gestures."

"Mine wasn't spontaneous," said Tom firmly. "Mine wasn't spontaneous at all. I thought it all out carefully. In the old days I wouldn't have gone with her but now I would and have. It isn't that I believe in church or in the usefulness of what the minister is saying. What I am affirming by that gesture as you call it is that the human being is more important than a religion one doesn't believe in. It's not even a question of selling one's soul since I don't believe that one has a soul to sell. It is simply saying that human happiness is more important than an hour or so spent in a museum. It is as simple as that."

"Or as complicated. And what about your own happiness?"

"My happiness? It doesn't affect my happiness one way or another."

"In that case."

"In that case what?"

"In that case there is nothing more to be said."

Tom was silent for a while and then he began again, "I don't understand exactly what it is you're saying."

"If you don't, then everything is all right, isn't it?"

71

I loved her, I still love her, he was thinking, and with sudden pain he remembered the two of them once driving out into the country in his car on a cold windy day. She had got out of the car to stand on a bridge looking down at a river which was snarling among broken rocks, and he had sat in his seat gazing at her in her brown coat with the fur collar, as she stood hunched at the wall staring down. She had looked so vulnerable, so small, as if she were a schoolgirl absorbed in a deep juvenile dream, while the water flowed past. Another time they had fallen asleep in a lay-by after driving back from Edinburgh and when, after he had wakened, he had gazed at her defenceless face he had felt the same intensity of protective feeling as if she were a fragile being that depended utterly on him. And now again the river was rushing among the hidden rocks and bearing him uncomprehendingly away with it.

"Perhaps it'll be all right," he said at last. "Perhaps she really is lonely." And he felt that he had been uncharitable, unjust. Who knew what went on on the depths of people's minds? Who knew what miseries this woman had endured? Maybe life had been hard on her, it wasn't, after all, natural to be unsociable. In general it could be said that people wanted to be liked if it was at all possible. And, as Vera had said, she wasn't a monster. No human being was a monster, or if they became monsters they weren't to blame. If one didn't believe that how could one continue as a teacher?

Vera is stronger than me, he thought, and not for the first time. There she sat sewing as if it all had been decided, as if an agreement had been arrived at, as if the embroidery were now all that mattered. She was right, he had surrendered an intellectual principle, in favour of the human, and why shouldn't he extend the same charity, if it was charity, to Ruth Donaldson Anything else would be inconsistent. He wondered if Vera had actually thought all that out, if she had put him in a box from the very beginning, and his mind had been too blunt to see it. Perhaps as well as being stronger than he was, she was also more intelligent, and it was the latter possibility that troubled him more. Perhaps her mind really was clearer than his, and she had seen more deeply than he had.

He went and sat beside her on the sofa and kissed the tip of her ear gently. "It will be all right," he said, "it might be a good idea after all."

She put down her sewing and replied, "I think it will. Why shouldn't it be?"

Their lips touched faintly. Directly ahead of him he could see the picture by Hockney of the blue staring swimming pool and he shivered. How could he ever have surrendered to fashion so completely as to have such a picture, so blatantly fierce, in his living room. Obviously the Dutch painters were the best. Their world was healthier, more human, less neurotic. And there was more light in them, clear and intellectual, falling about the domestic trivia of rooms with a mercy close to atonement.

12

THE LITTLE GIRL using a very long blackboard ruler for a stick hobbled about the floor, and talked to herself in senile tones.

"No one comes to visit me. No one ever comes to visit me. I sit here day after day and no one comes." She limped over to the black imaginary mirror of the blackboard and examined her face in it.

"I'm getting old. I can't get to the shops any more." She sat down on the high desk and forgetfully swung her legs, then steadied them.

"I'm tired." She thought for a minute and then said, "I'll go and make myself a cup of tea."

She got down from the desk, placing her legs, with the white socks on them on the floor and hobbled over to the plug in the wall to which she plugged an imaginary kettle, and waited.

"Sugar. I forgot about the sugar." She hobbled over to the cupboard and taking from it an invisible sugar bowl placed it on a desk.

"Milk," she said, and went over to the cupboard again.

"A cup."

"A spoon."

She walked back and forwards from the cupboard to the desk, and finally was satisfied.

She gazed down at the desk as if into a mirror and said, "I'm so old." She went over to the wall and returned with her imaginary kettle while tapping on the floor with her stick.

She poured imaginary water into an imaginary cup, put sugar and milk into it and then an imaginary tea bag, and then sat down on the high chair, placing the imaginary cup, which she stirred with an imaginary spoon, on the desk. She stared straight ahead of her while she was drinking.

"She's good," Vera was thinking. "I wish I could do that in so uninhibited a manner. But there was a stiffness in her nature which would not allow her to enter the mind and body of another person as this girl was doing. What direct innocent knowledge this little girl was showing: perhaps she had seen her granny and was imitating her.

The little girl had come to a halt in her little drama, not knowing what to do next.

She sat on the high seat awaiting instructions.

Vera stepped forward and stood in front of the class. "Someone is visiting you," she suggested. "Your son and his wife are visiting you. You are old. They want to put you in a home. Who wants to take the parts of the son and daughter?" Hands shot up: they all wanted to take part, they all wanted to be other than they were. She, on the contrary, was always herself, she wasn't a theatrical person, she didn't want to lose her sense of what she was. If the children had the sense or wisdom to ask me to take part, she thought, I wouldn't be able to do it, I would be too self conscious. And she loved them for their eagerness, their freshness, their willingness to obey her, their clean spotless faces. What lay behind these faces, what endless thoughts and resources? Her own mother would have been good at this, her careless theatrical mother, who had shone haphazardly on her in a colourful flurry like the sun passing in and out of her life. But her father would have been no good at it.

She picked a boy and a girl. They went to the door, knocked and the old lady told them to come in, her childish voice quavering.

"What do you want?" she said. "Do you want a cup of tea?"

"No thanks," they said almost in unison.

They stood about awkwardly and then the son said, "How are you, mother?" The two children stared at each other across the classroom floor.

"I'm fine," said the old woman. "No I'm not fine. I fell."

"Fell?"

"I fell when I was going down the stairs."

There was a pause.

"Mother, we were thinking that you should go away. This place is too . . ." the boy sought for a word, "too hard for you." He was not satisfied with the word and looked at Vera who said nothing but simply gazed back at him expressionlessly, neutrally.

"This place is not hard for me," said the old lady, her childish eyes blazing. She began to hammer the floor with her ruler. "This place is not too hard for me. It's not, it's not, it's not."

"But it is, mother. If you're falling downstairs. I think you should go to a home." The words came out with childish bluntness, without prevarication or disguise, with such a sudden brutal directness that Vera herself was suddenly shaken.

The child had forgotten that she was an old lady and was hammering on the floor in a tantrum.

The son said obsequiously and cunningly, "It would be for your own good," and his childish wife, standing beside him in her navy-blue uniform, repeated, "It would be for your own good."

"I won't go," said the old lady angrily. "I will phone my other son in Blackpool." Where had that come from, Vera wondered, why Blackpool?

The old lady hobbled over to a corner of the room where there was a large map of France and picked up an imaginary phone:

"Is that James? I should like to speak to my son James." She smiled triumphantly at the other two who were watching her, the boy rubbing one leg against the other.

"Is that you, James? Can I come and stay with you in Blackpool? I don't want to go to a home."

She appeared to listen and then turned back to the others and said, "He doesn't want me in Blackpool. He says his wife is pregnant." Again the word so nakedly spoken shocked Vera and she almost intervened but against her better instincts did nothing. "This is getting out of control," she thought. "What are they going to say next? What?"

The old woman hobbled back to the high desk and the son thrust at her cruelly. "You see? You'll have to go to a home. You can't stay here. You're always falling down."

"I'm not, I'm not, I'm not. I fell down once but I'm not always falling down." And she screamed a high-pitched scream.

"That's too loud," said Vera breaking the spell. "You'll disturb the teacher in the next room." They stared at her as if they had come out of a dream. "More quietly," she said. Why couldn't they do what they were told? Why must they always take advantage? Why couldn't they be like herself, obedient, keeping to the script?

The silence prolonged itself. "Well, go on," she said, "what are you waiting for?"

But they couldn't at first quite get back into the rhythm which they had earlier established. It was as if they had returned to being themselves again, and they couldn't resume their ageing flesh.

"I think you should go to a home," said the boy without conviction.

"No," said the old lady.

They were becalmed, not knowing how to proceed.

"You say to her," said Vera in a cold calm voice, "that she just has to go. You tell her that. There is no other way."

"You have to go to a home," said the son, "there is no other way."

Suddenly the old lady began to cry. "But you're my son," she wailed, "why do I have to go to a home?"

"It's because we have six children and we can't take you," said the wife mercilessly, neat and clean in her uniform.

"I could stay with you," said the old lady.

"No," said the wife, "we have six children. And two of them sleep in the attic, already. And the house is full of toys and books. And anyway my father won't allow you." She stopped, suddenly realising what she had said, and then added, "My husband . . . he won't allow you."

The old lady began to talk to herself, "After all I did for you. I wouldn't put you in a home. If you were old I wouldn't put you in a home. I would give you a room. I would give you even a small room." And she gazed down from her high chair into a small room imaginary and distant. "It would have dolls in it. And books. And a rocking chair," she added with sudden inspiration.

"You have to go," said the son, now totally obsessed. "You're always falling down and you'll have to go. You're always crying all the time. People are fed up of your crying. You're making everybody sad. And I have to catch the bus every Thursday to come and see you. I'm fed up visiting you. You're too old."

His wife nodded in agreement but the old woman fiercely replied: "I'm staying here. You can't put me out. This is my house. Go away. Go away from here."

"That's right," said Vera to herself. "You tell them to go away. You tell them to go away, you stay where you are. Don't let them put you out. You stay and read your books, don't go out of the house for them."

The honesty of children, Vera thought. "I have to take the bus to see you every Thursday." When we grow up we hide everything. Why can't we be as honest as the children? You're trying to take my husband away from me, old woman, you're making him pity you. Perhaps you never had a break-in at all, perhaps it was all an invention. You're trying to get your son back, that's what you're doing, old woman. You may not even realise it yourself but it's what you are doing all the same. And he for his part goes on with his claptrap about the church. You on the other hand have the defenceless cunning and the selfishness of the old. You're playing on his better instincts, you're making him into a slushy humanitarian without principles. All these trains, fathers waving out of the smoke, you're putting that into his mind. The days of the tenements are over, this world we're living in is not that world any longer. It's not a world of people huddling together for warmth like cattle in the cold, drinking, fornicating, gossiping at corners. We are all orphans just like Jane Eyre. We are all sitting at our own little table in a large draughty world. You are betraying, Tom, the strictness of the intellect.

As she looked at the imaginary stage, where the children were still fixed in their poses, she knew that it wasn't a stage at all, it was a schoolroom floor, bare and unpolished and ancient, not the wooden O but the wooden world, the world which is the world of all of us, where our poor footsteps echo.

"You make me come here on the bus every Thursday." Their eyes, pagan and fierce and innocent and sincere, gazed at her like the eyes of the doll that she had kept in order to . . . in order to do what? To populate the nursery forever abandoned, or forever kept? The doll which was a link with her childhood, with her mother and father, or which was a substitute for both? Jane out in the rain and the storm, orphaned, alone, in the reality of the nineteenth century and not in any theatre.

"All right then," said the son, "all right then, you stay where you are. But I won't be back on the bus on Thursday. You

78

have to learn to live alone." Her mind was beating remorselessly and steadily like a white stick against the floor, like a white stalk.

The play was over. The actors had all gone. The stick had become a ruler again. The children had turned back into children again, her loved obedient ones, sitting upright in their desks, so clean, so submissive. And her bowels were moved with love for them. My bowels are moved as in the Bible, in the Old Testament. They are the promise and the bond, the rainbow in the sky. If only ... if only ...

"Now," she said, "you may read silently for the rest of the period." If only ...

13

TOM STOOD IN front of the class, the copy of *The Waste Land* in his hand while directly in front of him through the window he could see the rowan tree, slim and light, still bearing its berries. It seemed to him that he was in the wrong place, that there was some other place where he could more profitably be at that moment, though he couldn't think where it was. Not certainly with his legs curled up in a narrow canoe, not climbing dark stairs to a lustful rendezvous, with a bald spot in the middle of his forehead.

"Eliot," he said, "is undoubtedly one of our greatest poets," and the words echoed hollowly in the room. One of our greatest poets, what did that mean? It was like saying, Tide is certainly one of our best washing powders, its suds billow more fluently and more abundantly than those of other washing powders.

"He achieves his effects by oblique means," he continued, "and in this is different from for instance . . ." Well, who for instance? Cowper? Burns? Thomas Campbell? Dorothy Hemans? And again the image came into his mind, sharp and clear, of that old woman, fat and red faced, walking down the road by herself, her big red hands clutching a shopping bag, while all the time she was talking to herself, a big waddling doll, now and again stopping in front of shop windows and looking into them as if they were mirrors.

They were all—all the girls, fresh-faced and earnest—writing it down in their notebooks. *Eliot is certainly one of our greatest poets.* If he is not one of our greatest poets then what is he? What to be precise is he? "Nothing. What is that noise under the door? Nothing. Nothing will come of nothing." There is a sense in which the rowan tree communicates joy, it returns every year, laden with its berries, indomitable, repetitive, its roots sunk in the earth, fighting for their place as once in the tenements people fought for their place, sang, laughed, cried, were alive, drunken, spontaneous, remarkable.

"Thus," he continued, for their eyes were fixed on him as if he were their guru, their oracle. But what were they really thinking of, behind that bland apparently interested facade?

"Thus we have to consider what poetry is, and in what way or ways Eliot is a new kind of poet, a revolutionary poet. We have to wonder for instance why he is so esoteric" (no, better change that word) "difficult, why he returns again and again to books, preferring to quote rather than to . . ."

And while his mouth exuded words, his eyes, fixed on what was going on outside the window, saw a big yellow and blue machine with a long neck like that of a dinosaur scooping up earth and rubble from the road, and sitting in the machine was a young man who was leaning forward, naked and brown above the waist, to see what the machine was doing. And it suddenly occurred to Tom to ask himself what the young man was thinking of, what his thoughts truly were at that particular moment. With great intensity he tried to put his own mind into that of the young man, and was repulsed again and again by a blinding darkness, like a star so faint that it cannot pierce the night. He made attempt after attempt to think of himself as bare and tanned in that machine as it dug up the road on an autumn day, but he could feel nothing, not the controls, not the breeze on his bare back, not the sun flickering warmly off the steel. And it came to him with utter certainty, as he watched the young man and the other one who was holding on to a bouncing pneumatic drill, that he didn't have any idea at all what the lad was thinking of, that he was as distant from the world of the young man as he was from the world of the pupils he was teaching, that never again would he be able to understand that world and not simply understand it but feel it and rest within it, happy and negligent, as if he really belonged to it naturally and without effort.

"Eliot," he heard himself saying, "can be compared with Picasso for he uses the same techniques. In the same way as in a Picasso painting we can see apparently unrelated images, such as heads of horses, candles, faces with three eyes, so we can find in Eliot as well images which apparently seem set down at random and without order." But what did they know about Picasso and in order to tell them about Picasso he would have to . . . There was no end to the complexity and interrelatedness of the world—

everything in the world must be talked of in terms of everything else. Except perhaps for the rowan which we do not dare to see as it really is, the rowan tree which is definitely not a system of quotations, unless it was quoting itself endlessly, but certainly not quoting all the other rowan trees that had lived through summer and autumn until they had died and been renewed again.

What was that young man thinking of as he so proudly and arrogantly manœuvred his machine along the road, looking back now and again, and whistling as he did so to make sure that the machine was under his control, that it was gathering together all the rubbish and depositing it where it should be deposited, that its long neck was digging into the ground as a swan into water, that it was fulfilling its proper function in the repair of the road over which so many cars would soon pass to their proper destinations. And the young man was thinking, must be thinking. Well, what were his thoughts? Was he thinking that last night he had managed after all to get that girl without mercy, that he had finally wiped the smile off her face, that he lay afterwards in his bed sleeping the sleep of the tired, and that today he was whistling because he had accomplished what he had set out to accomplish? Or was he thinking only of the machine itself, of the autumn day, of the breeze on his back? And how did the world appear to him? Certainly not distant, certainly not a series of quotations, but immediate rather, the machine immediate, the air immediate and cool, the work he was doing immediate and necessary, his hands there in the actual world clutching, manœuvring, so that if he had been a poet his poetry would have been immediate and without theory, he would grasp the real world as directly and roughly as the machine was doing.

But stop a moment, Tom told himself. For he recognised that he was doing what Eliot had done, that is associating the young man wholly with sex, the young man carbuncular, climbing the dark stairs for a quick piece of intercourse; that to him as to Eliot the young man was not a real being but a caricature, not to be distinguished clearly from the machine, someone who was not really worth taking notice of, someone who had not been seen, for it was assumed that he had nothing important to say or feel. And there in front of him, what were these girls thinking of as they took their notes. What was their world—the desks immediate, the pen or pencil immediate, their clothes immediate and in fact they far more able to approach that young man and talk to him as he whistled from his lordly position on that machine than he himself was, who once had come from a world not all that different from that of the young man.

"In earlier poetry," he continued, "we don't have this sort of difficulty or at least not to this extent. For what Eliot is doing is this, he is referring to the past, he is continually evoking it as a part of the present, juxtaposing images of order such as those of the Elizabethan against the meaningless present." But, he thought to himself, he was also leaving out the sweating seething world of the real Elizabethans, the world of the streets, of the ballad makers, of those who sold their wares at markets, of the dagger and the murder and the theft.

"But before I go on about that I should like to talk for a moment about fertility symbolism."

He drew a deep breath. How could he even begin on that, Frazer and the rest of them? The new leader pursuing the old leader in the dark wood, ready to kill him, as the new stag took on the old stag so that on an autumn slope one might find the two of them dead, their antlers locked together among the stones, their eyes glazed.

They were so docile, so quiet, taking all of it down while, outside, the young man was casually manipulating the machine.

The young immediate stag in the cool of the morning. No, he thought, I can't go on with this. This is not of their world: they are obedient and they listen but this doesn't belong to them, this belongs only to the world of those who have left the immediate, who have brooded over it till finally it has become a haze, a mist of the morning.

Why should they listen to this story of those who have seen nothingness, who have walked alone in the middle of London listening to the dead sound from the church clock, who have hollow eyes and hollow hearts. What is this to them? For they don't have hollow eyes and hollow hearts, they are full of hope, ready to set out into the real world of all of us: they have not yet suffered this dispossession.

Why, he asked himself, was Leicester not carbuncular, or Elizabeth or Tristan or for that matter Iseult? No, they must not be allowed to be carbuncular, but the young man must be made so, for the plot demands it, the symmetries require it.

He shut the book abruptly and said, "I think we'll leave Eliot for a while." He left the room and went briskly in search of the plays of Sean O'Casey, walking very confidently and surely as if he were a train that had come at last out of a dark tunnel and was picking up speed again, and would later enter a station where there was movement, people passing and repassing, on different errands, the bustle of life itself which cannot be denied, cannot be avoided, which in all conscience cannot be other than it is, unpredictable, spontaneous, untidy, and in some sense inexplicable and finally perhaps holy.

14

ON THE EVENING of the dinner Tom went to pick up Mrs Murphy to take her to the house: Ruth Donaldson had her own car. He left his mother nervously sitting in the living room (while Vera was cooking in the kitchen) and now and again checking that her watch was right. She was wearing a brown dress for the occasion while round her neck was a necklace of imitation pearls. The weather had broken and there was a little rain when he set out; the leaves on the road were wet and soggy and it looked for the first time as if winter would soon be coming. The breathless pose in which the trees had rested for so long was slightly disturbed and occasionally a slight wind got up, dishevelling the few leaves that still remained on the branches. It was beginning to darken earlier, and street lamps were going on for the first time.

His car drew up in front of the tenement and he got out and walked into the close at the back of which were piled a lot of cardboard boxes which had probably been stored there by the shopkeeper next door. They looked soggy as if the rain had been getting at them, and indeed there was some water in the close itself. He climbed the wooden stairs slowly, hearing a step creak now and again: he looked out of a window which was set in the wall halfway up and thought for a moment of a "broadbacked figure playing the flute": he smiled wryly. But all he saw was the rope and posts for hanging up washing, and round the sides a small narrow area which had been dug up and in which some flowers, now wilting, had been planted.

He pressed the bell at the door and waited. Finally footsteps came to the door, and there in front of him was Mrs Murphy. He hadn't known quite what to expect but this brisk figure, dressed in a flowery frock, was perhaps not quite what he had pictured beforehand. Splay-legged and seeming to move like a sailor on a plunging deck she preceded him into the room.

"Would you take a seat?" she said to him and it was as if she were some socialite whom perhaps she had seen on a film in the past, and whom she was now imitating: the words came out like a false echo of a language that was not natural to her. He felt suddenly depressed as if something dreadful was about to happen, a dinner party composed of people who would be, as it were, reciting words that they did not mean and watching each other like malicious momently-animated dolls. "I won't be long," said Mrs Murphy and then turning at the door she said, "Thank you very much for the invitation" and it to him that she was simpering. It occurred to him that she was seeing him as a person from a class higher than her own, a teacher, and that she was therefore trying to make an impression. God, he thought, don't let her offer me a glass of sherry.

He waited while she readied herself, and looked around the room, studying the photographs on the mantelpiece and the wall. One showed a wedding in which a young girl, with knife poised, was about to cut a three-tiered wedding cake while beside her there stood smiling a thick-set slightly older man who looked like a boxer. In another picture there was a young soldier who was smiling sunnily, his diced cap aslant and negligent on his head.

The room was overcrowded like the one in their own early flat but the ceiling was higher and stained as if it had broken out into a variety of brown measles. He wondered whether this had been caused by condensation over a long period. How old were these houses anyway? He speculated idly that they must be at least a hundred years old and that before Mrs Murphy there had been a succession of tenants, each of them entering the flat with the eternal hope that springs in the human breast of assiduously transforming old rooms to their own desires.

As she entered, having put a long fur coat over her frock, he immediately stood up. Where had she got the fur coat from anyway? She must be richer than he had thought, or perhaps her sons sent her money regularly. There was even a touch of lipstick on her lips.

"Are you ready then, Mrs Murphy?" he asked. "I'm so glad you could come," and again he heard but this time from himself words that seemed superficial and without feeling, because he could think of little else to say to her, the distance between their two worlds was now so great.

"Yes, I'm ready," she answered adding, "It was so good of you to have me." She checked that her key was in her handbag and

86

after she had shut the door they made their way down the stairs, Tom telling her that it was wetter than it had been in previous weeks and she as if for a moment reverting to her early Irish world—but perhaps only repeating the ordinary trivialities of conversation—saying that the farmers would be glad of the rain. It seemed to him that, as he opened the door of the car for her and she stepped into it, clutching her handbag, she looked up at the windows of the tenement briefly as if hoping that some of the neighbours would see her as they peered out from behind their curtains, wondering where she was going and who the toff was that had called on her. But in fact when he followed her brief avid glance he saw no one.

On the way to the house she chattered away about the weather and he asked her how long she had been in the town and what she thought of it.

"I don't mind it," she said. "I wouldn't go back to Ireland now. Did your mother tell you that I come from Ireland? Well, I do. But I wouldn't go back there. The brothers want me to go back but I wouldn't." And Tom imagined a whole host of brothers, wearing dungarees and standing on their crofts, pleading with her to return to the land of Erin which she should never have left in the first place while behind it all there was the music of Ireland, and a singer in a green dress repeated some such word as Mavourneen over and over again, at the same time plucking the strings of a harp.

By the time they had reached the house however she had withdrawn into herself again, clutching her handbag tightly in the seat beside him, as if at any moment she expected that someone would take it away from her. It was darkening appreciably when they stepped out of the car, he opening the door for her: and she remarked, though perhaps she couldn't make out the object of her compliment very well: "It's a lovely house you have here."

"It's not bad," said Tom.

She paused for a moment below the light which fell over the threshold, her fur coat heavy and dark and her handbag in her hand. Then she turned to him and for the first time a mischievous smile illuminated her face below the white light:

"Well, into the britch," she said, surprisingly, and Tom saw her in a sudden flash as she might once have been, a young Irish girl arriving for the first time at the "big house" somewhere in a big city.

"Up the intellectuals, Mrs Murphy," he said under his breath as he followed her into the house.

15

Ruth Donaldson who did not believe in dressing for dinner—and was wearing black slacks and a yellow jersey—sat in front of the fire, a whisky beside her on the long rectangular coffee table. It was ten minutes to seven and she would leave at twenty past. She felt nervous and unsure, unused to going out, though she had talked to Vera and knew who was going to be there. As she drank her whisky, she wished that she hadn't agreed to go to dinner at all, and felt more than any anticipation her own clumsiness and resentment. If the others wanted to dress up, let them, she would show them what she was, unadorned and without pretence, an awkward person whom no one much wanted or had wanted up till now. The raw whisky comforted her, and she poured herself another one. Like many other lonely people, she was finding that drink was the only antidote to her ever-present sense of isolation, not the philosophy of Plato, nor even the TV or radio. Without it, she would have felt even more deserted and miserable than she actually was and her imperative desires would have been even more unbearable. Sometimes at night before going to bed, she would remove all her clothes and look in the mirror at her heavy breasts, unused, infertile, as if she were gazing at some other being on whom she had all the pity in the world. Yet she did not know whom, on these barren nocturnal occasions, she was offering herself to: her desire was unfocussed like the eyes of a drunk. All she knew was that her desire was towards some other being who would accept her as she was, her heaviness, her ugliness, her tortured hating mind. For she knew deep within herself that isolation is the worst of fortunes, and that without at least one other person, there was no life at all, only existence.

She wondered about Vera Mallow? Why had she invited her? Did she have some reason that she hadn't told her. Her mother-in-law was to be there, as was a Mrs Murphy and Vera's husband whom she had never spoken to but whom she considered a rather wet liberal type who preened himself on his fastidiousness. Vera, however, was different: she had a colder more realistic mind and did nothing without real motive. She sensed that with Vera she was in the presence of someone not unlike herself, though prettier in a cold nun-like way. But why had she invited her? Her story about material for a Joseph project was clearly suspect for there was little that she could tell her that she did not already know, and in any case what possible time would there be for discussion of such a subject, during a dinner when there were others as well. No, there was more to it than that. And with the second whisky in her hand she speculated.

It wasn't simply that Vera had invited her to a dinner where there only would be herself and her husband, for there would also be her mother-in-law and Mrs Murphy. Was there some meaning hidden there? It was as if Vera were trying to tell her something which she did not wish to speak straight out. Did Vera therefore know something of her own history? Had she specially chosen her for some work that she could do, implying that if this work were done then a closer relationship would follow?

She looked around her at the flat—the sofa and chairs covered in red, the reproductions of Van Gogh and Gauguin on the walls, the opposite ones being papered in red and black respectively; and she imagined Vera sitting in front of her, icy and remote, her hands folded on her lap, and the desire was so strong in her that she felt her chest reddening and her face flushing.

I need someone else, she almost screamed, I need someone, almost anyone, I cannot go on like this. Without any attachment at all, what are we? Nothing. We are floating about anchorless in the world, ships adrift in the sea, like the ones she could see, if she had drawn the curtains, out in the bay in front of her. We are ghosts walking about the world, bodiless and without weight. If we are not to hate the world, we need someone, if we are not to succumb to violence and evil, and spiritual death.

She felt herself as a symbol of a definite truth, naked and vulnerable, looking in at the fires of others but condemned to stay outside, snarling in the darkness. I have been given nothing in my whole life, she thought, nothing. I was never loved, not even my mother loved me, she used me but she did not love me.

I must break into the circle somewhere somehow. If I don't break into the circle I shall die.

But how to break into the circle? That was the question. And as she thought about it, the second whisky finished, and the glass beside her on the table she thought she knew what she had to do, she thought she understood why Vera had invited her. It came to her as in a vision which the whisky had created and clarified, a vision so pure that it illuminated her totally in its light; she saw herself as a weapon being used, a pistol or revolver there on the table, a servant whose obedience is accepted without thought. It was so obvious that she couldn't understand how she hadn't thought of it before. It lay manifestly evident before her, as if under the bareness of electric light.

She debated whether she should take another whisky but decided against it for after all she had to drive her car and though the Mallows' house wasn't very far away anything could happen. In any case she hadn't had much food, and she had learned from experience that too much whisky on an empty stomach wasn't good for her.

The clock showed quarter past seven and she rose from her seat, and, coatless, switched off the lights, shut the door and walked to her car. She drove carefully among the multitudes of lights to the Mallows, feeling nervous and slightly feverish, though less so than before she had taken her two whiskies. The rain beat steadily on the windscreen, monotonously cleared by the wiper, and the wind was higher than she had realised it was while she was sitting in her flat.

PART TWO

1

THEY SAT AWKWARDLY on chairs and sofa about the living room, Vera, Tom, Mrs Murphy, Ruth Donaldson and Mrs Mallow.

"Well then," said Vera brightly, "now that we're all here I think we should have a drink."

She went over to the sideboard and Tom was surprised to see four or five bottles there: she must have bought them the previous day for he couldn't remember their having been there before.

"Ruth?" she said.

"I'll take a whisky. No water, please."

"Whisky. No water," Vera repeated. And then, "Tom, perhaps you could help me."

"Fine," said Tom. "I always knew bartending was my destiny." Mrs Murphy laughed, and the others smiled.

"Mrs Murphy?" said Vera. It occurred to Tom that she had left his mother to the last and this bothered him slightly.

"I'll take a drop of Martini if you have it. A small drop."

"Lemonade?"

"That would be all right."

Vera handed her the glass and then looked inquiringly at her mother-in-law.

"Nothing for me," said Mrs Mallow, turning apologetically to the others. "I don't drink, you see."

"Come on mother," Tom pleaded, "just for tonight. You don't have to drive or anything. You don't have to leave the house. Now if it was Ruth here or even Mrs Murphy." Finally she was persuaded to take a lemonade, Vera poured out a small Martini for herself, while Tom took a whisky.

They sat in their chairs with their drinks in their hands and there was a silence till Tom remarked,

"Well, it's good to be sitting here and not thinking about school."

"You're perfectly right," said Ruth. "Mrs Murphy and your mother here don't know what we have to put up with."

She drank her whisky rapidly, nervously, while Mrs Murphy

looked at her and thought, "Funny she doesn't wear a better dress than that. She's an odd one, that."

"What do you do then?" she asked.

"I teach. That's what I do. For my sins."

"For her sins is right," said Tom. "She teaches Religious Education. We don't have her problems."

"Oh," said Mrs Murphy.

Tom's mother, as if embarrassed that she had contributed nothing to the conversation so far, suddenly remarked, "Tom teaches English, you know." The words, so shyly offered, hung nakedly in the room as if unconnected with what had gone before, and Ruth Donaldson who had turned to look at Mrs Mallow turned away again, as if abruptly dismissing her.

"It's like this," she said, "Religious Education is a twilight subject, I'm afraid, Mrs Murphy. No one is interested in it. It is taught as a sop to the consciences of education departments. When I came here first I was offered all sorts of cooperation but when I actually arrived what did I find? I found a dull room with some of the window panes smashed, children who aren't interested in anything I have to offer, and no money available for buying books or maps or anything else. One would have thought that there would have been enough hypocrisy in existence to provide decent working conditions and material, but no. There's not even enough of that."

She felt quite happy, the centre of attention for the moment, in that room where she had a number of listeners, and at the same time a glass in her hand, the whisky of which she had already drunk.

"Another?" said Vera, noticing, as she sat slightly apart from the others in her white dress.

"Well, if you like. If you're sure it's no trouble."

What sort of woman was this, Mrs Murphy was wondering, a religious teacher drinking whisky all the time. Mrs Mallow sat smiling on them all, saying nothing.

"I'm sure," said Tom, "that Mrs Murphy and my mother here will find your problems of interest."

"Bugger," thought Ruth savagely, taking the whisky from Vera, and touching her hand slightly as she did so.

Vera gazed at her enigmatically.

96

"Do you come from Ireland then?" Ruth asked Mrs Murphy. "I thought with a name like that you might come from Ireland."

"I do. I come from Connemara."

"Do you go back there often?"

"Not now. I used to go back there but not now."

There was another silence and Tom glancing at his mother said,

"Are you sure that lemonade is all you want?"

"Yes, Tom, I'm fine." Her face retained the same fixed smile as if she had decided to put it on with her dress.

"My mother," he went on, "my mother and I at one time used to live in a tenement in Edinburgh. We met a lot of Irish people there. Very likeable people too. I remember when my father was in hospital . . . but mother will tell you."

"What was that, Tom?"

"You remember when my father was in hospital, mother?"

"Oh yes. They made a collection you see. They brought it to me. Was that it Tom?" she asked anxiously.

"That's right mother. But you didn't tell it all. This tall Irishman, slightly drunk, came to the door with this collection and he said to my mother, 'It's just a little drop of money.' And when we opened the envelope there were fifteen pounds in it. And yet they didn't have much money themselves. You see, the Irish are very generous—not much respect for law and order, mind you, if you'll excuse me Mrs Murphy—but warm and generous. My mother loved it there didn't you, mother?"

"Yes, Tom." The centre of attention, she was red with embarrassment, and found it difficult to speak.

"I would say they are like that," said Mrs Murphy comfortably. Ruth Donaldson glanced contemptuously at the three of them and then winked at Vera who was saying nothing but watching everybody, the Martini in her glass hardly touched.

"Bitch," thought Tom, noticing the wink. "Warm heartedness is a great virtue. Perhaps some of us have lost it, that sense of community. I sometimes wonder whether the middle classes may not have lost it." He turned to Vera who smiled but didn't speak.

"Oh I wouldn't say that," said Ruth Donaldson. "Warm heartedness can be found in all classes, I would say." Her whisky glass was empty again. "It is not an exclusive possession of what we may call, for lack of a better phrase, the lower classes. I would have said that it was a function of the personality who either had or hadn't got it." She was puzzled a bit by the end of the sentence which seemed to have got a little out of control and added,

"I think the other view is a sort of sentimentalism, myself."

"Have you ever read O'Casey?" Tom asked furiously, ready for an argument.

"I have and my opinion remains unchanged."

"If you're saying that the people in the big houses are as warm hearted as the people in the tenements," Mrs Murphy suddenly intervened," then you're wrong, begging your pardon. I clean the stairs for them and I know. They stick to their pennies, the same people. You find a rich man and you'll find a man who sticks to his pennies, and what's the end of it all, six feet of earth, that's what I always say." She looked around her with satisfaction.

Ruth Donaldson was about to say something when Vera interposed.

"If you would all like to go into dinner now. You must be starving. Take your drinks in with you. Ruth? Do you want another one? Anyone else?"

Without speaking, Ruth handed over her glass to be filled and they went into the dining room.

Tom sat at the head of the table, Vera and Ruth facing each other, Mrs Mallow and Mrs Murphy also facing each other.

The shining table had been laid, with two candles in the middle, red napkins in a vase and the best plates and cutlery. The curtains had been drawn but as they were entering Tom heard the wind and rain beating against the window and said, "There seems to be a bit of a storm. The weather has broken."

In the dusk of the room—for the electric light had been switched off—he saw the candles trembling and casting white circles on the table. It occurred to him that tall and pure as they were they would shed grease on the plates below.

They began with a clear soup which Ruth Donaldson gulped as if she were not at all interested in food while Mrs Murphy and Tom's mother sipped theirs slowly.

Tom said, "Vera is a very good cook. But you mustn't imagine I get this sort of food every day." There was some laughter in which however Ruth Donaldson pointedly did not join, keeping her large head bent over her plate.

Now and again Tom would glance at Vera who hardly entered the conversation but attended to her duties as hostess competently and quietly. She never felt embarrassed by her own silence, but thought of it as a demonstration of power: it was the weakest people who talked the most. Tom wondered what she was up to, and couldn't make up his mind: perhaps if he got a chance between courses he might ask her. Meanwhile, cool and self-possessed as always, she did exactly what was expected of her but at the same time contributed nothing beyond that as if she had carefully measured out what her responsibility was and was adhering to its limits. The thought suddenly came to him, she is saying nothing because whatever happens I shall not then be able to blame her. She will be able to say, "I didn't cause any of it. I did what was required of me. I was precisely as generous as I ought to have been. And in any case it was your idea that Mrs Murphy should be invited. Or are you suggesting that she isn't suitable for company."

He gazed at the candles as if with a premonition that in some way they were connected with whatever might happen. What I need, he thought, is to get drunk. That's what I need. Holding all this together is beginning to grow too much for me. The centre is beginning to crack. His mother sat smiling in her chair. She is hating this, he thought, she is hating every minute. She is not at ease, she has nothing to say, she is too embarrassed to speak. And yet we should all be happy round the table, we should feel a communal sense of contentment: why then don't we? Is it because all human relationships are impossible, the nudge, the sharp points, the egos starving or triumphant, the love that is never sufficient. And at that moment he glanced up and saw Ruth Donaldson's eyes fixed on his wife with such a naked desire that he almost fainted with the force of it.

He took the bottle of wine and poured some out for everybody including his mother (though she protested) and a large amount for himself. So it's war he thought. War to the death and he gazed at Ruth Donaldson with rage and hatred.

"I hope this won't harm you after the whisky," he said with barbed solicitousness.

"Not at all," she challenged him across the table. "You should have given your mother more."

"I won't drink even this much," said his mother quietly.

"As a matter of fact she doesn't need it," Tom pursued mercilessly, "she doesn't have to teach religion."

Point one to me, he thought savagely, as he saw Ruth Donaldson turn pale.

"Are you all right, Mrs Murphy?"

"I'm fine. To tell you the truth I never mix my drinks myself."

So we're taking sides, then let us: let us throw caution to the winds and enjoy ourselves. Let's choose our teams, the rest of us against you and Vera. Or is Vera perhaps being neutral? So far she hasn't committed herself to either side, she has remained in the dressing room, not a hair out of place. Or perhaps she has committed herself to Ruth Donaldson, and that is what all this is about. It was going to be very hard to prevent the table from becoming a battlefield, and maybe it wasn't worth making the effort. Who the hell cared about Ruth Donaldson anyway? His own mother had a better claim to mercy than she had.

He drank his wine and watched as Vera put the duckling and orange on the plates.

Suddenly his mother said, "The other day Mrs Murphy and I took a walk up to the castle. Have you ever been there, Miss Donaldson? It's a very old castle. You can see the whole town from it. You can see this house from it, can't you, Mrs Murphy?"

"You can that. You can see the whole town."

"And do you like the town then," Ruth Donaldson asked sweetly. "Do you like staying here?" And she subtly emphasised the last word as if she meant by it not simply the town but the house in which they were sitting.

"It's very different from Edinburgh."

"In what way, Mrs Mallow?"

"Well, it's smaller. And there's the sea."

"Ah, the sea. Of course. That must make a considerable difference. All the difference there is." And she drank some wine.

"The sea must make a lot of difference, wouldn't you say, Mrs

Murphy? Coming from Connemara you must miss the sea, the boats and the rocks and all that."

"I don't know. Would you be missing the sea yourself?" said Mrs Murphy and it seemed to the delighted Tom that she had deliberately exaggerated her Irishness. Good for you, ould woman, he muttered under his breath, and all the Mrs Murphies of the world. May your God go with you.

"Of course," he said aloud, "it is possible that Miss Donaldson doesn't deal much with the sea, apart from the Sea of Galilee. Do you, Miss Donaldson?"

"Not even that one, Mr Mallow."

If this were the Last Supper, thought Tom a little drunkenly, I should go and kiss her as our betrayer. I should perhaps ask her to change this wine back to water, if she can do it. Bloody old hag, and bitch of the first water, or for that matter the second and third and all successive ones.

So she had brought her hate into this room, her frustration, her hypocritical divinity, her loneliness and her sorrow.

Ruth Donaldson drank some more wine rapidly and then said as if to no one in particular:

"I suppose there can be as much sentimentalism about the sea as there can be about tenements. I was brought up in one myself but I can't say that I liked it. And as for the sea I know that there's the Masefield syndrome and all that but I have always thought that there was nothing interesting about a lot of uneventful water."

(Good stuff for the peasants this, thought Tom furiously. "The Masefield syndrome, would that be something like an airport now. How deep the ould one is.")

"I don't know about that," said Mrs Murphy. "The sea can be very pretty on a calm day. My husband liked the sea and he missed it too. He used to go trout fishing when we were in Connemara. He was very keen on the fishing." And she looked defiantly around her as if she were defending his sacred memory against attack.

At that moment to Tom's chagrin his mother dropped her fork but before he could do anything about it Vera had picked it up. His mother, flustered and red in the face, said nothing but Ruth Donaldson, not one to miss a weakness in one of his allies, remarked "That wine must be stronger than we thought." His mother looked down at her plate like a corrected schoolgirl, and Tom shaking with rage thrust again at Ruth Donaldson,

"We're so glad you like it so much," pointing to her empty glass. "Would you like some more?"

"Yes, please," blatantly impudent.

"They do say," said Mrs Murphy, "that winos are worse than alcoholics. I have heard that said," and she gazed around her with a brisk innocent air.

The candles fluttered a little in the draught which came from the window and Mrs Mallow, as if her inhibitions were beginning to wear off with the wine, remarked,

"It's not often you see candles on a table nowadays, though you see them in hotels. Do you remember, Tom, that hotel where they had the candles?"

"Yes," Tom replied, furious that she was offering Ruth Donaldson some of their history.

"Oh, where was that?" Ruth Donaldson asked in the same sweet tone as before. "Was that in Edinburgh?"

"It was," replied Mrs Mallow eagerly. "It was in a hotel in Edinburgh though I can't remember its name now. Tom took me to dinner there one night and I think we had duckling and oranges there too. Tom liked it very much, didn't you Tom?"

Before Tom could answer Ruth Donaldson probed, "Oh, did you go out to dinner often then? It's nice to see such close affection between son and mother. And rather unusual." She paused. "I must say that I didn't like my own mother very much. She was a very difficult woman, but I'm sure you're not that, Mrs Mallow. She was always telling me to do this and that, and not to be out too late. But I suppose one must understand that."

"I would imagine that you would show great understanding," said Tom recklessly. She looked at him across the table, murderously. "I only meant," Tom continued in a voice that was as sweet as her own, "that your knowledge of religion and your obvious belief in it would help you to deal with other people in a charitable manner."

"Religion has nothing to do with it," Ruth Donaldson replied bluntly as if she had discarded caution and etiquette.

"Oh I thought religion might have something to do with it. I

102

thought it taught us about love. But perhaps I am mistaken. They make so many new discoveries nowadays."

Vera's eyes were moving from Tom to Ruth and back again as if she were at a tennis match but at no time did she make any effort to speak. What are you playing at, Tom thought savagely, cursing under his breath. What have you set up here? But before he could pursue what had now become an open argument between himself and Ruth Donaldson, Mrs Murphy said:

"We have a good young priest here, you know. He's very good to the old people. He goes round in his car and he visits the Protestants too. He's very kind."

Ruth Donaldson gazed at her in disgust and then suddenly said, abruptly, "I wonder if I could go to the bog for a moment."

"This way," said Vera, and the two of them left the dining room, leaving Tom alone with his mother and Mrs Murphy.

"She doesn't seem to be very well," said Mrs Murphy smiling at him. "Perhaps she's had too much to drink. She seems a very unhappy young woman." Not unhappy, thought Tom, simply wicked, evil. Unhappiness if it is unhappiness can cause evil and wickedness. There will be trouble before we get her out of the house.

"Don't you worry," he told Mrs Murphy. "We are very glad to see you."

"Tom got these plates as a wedding present," said Mrs Mallow casting around for something to say. "He and Vera have been married for five years now."

"Oh?"

Words, words, words, thought Tom. What use is language after all? Here we all are in the middle of an unspoken struggle, each bringing to it his or her own troubles and thoughts, and our words pass like ghosts about the battlefield. He poured out some more wine for himself and drank it quickly. Bugger it all, he thought, is this what Vera and I have been avoiding in the past, all these tears and bitternesses, scenes like these. Did we stay alone with each other in protection against the barbs and stings of this sort of painful reality. As he looked at his mother, he saw that she was staring down at her plate while Mrs Murphy was pretending as hard as she could to be studying a picture of a fawn in a green wood that was hanging on the wall.

Vera and Ruth Donaldson came back in, and Tom stared with loathing at the latter's flat slab-like face. They continued to eat their duckling in silence for a while.

Without any warning, Ruth Donaldson began where she had left off, "Religion? What is it anyway? How does it help? I mean, look at us. Old, ugly, happy or unhappy, what does it do for us? Tell me that. Can anyone tell me that? My own mother was a religious woman but that didn't prevent her from being a bitch. Look at you," she said to Mrs Murphy, "I'm sure you're a good Catholic. I'm sure you're interested in candles and the Mass and things like that but how does that help us in the end. Can anyone tell me that?" And her sick eyes fastened on them.

"Oh I wouldn't say that," said Mrs Murphy. "I wouldn't say that at all. I mean we don't just believe in candles do we? Religion can help you to bear your grief. When my own husband died I don't know what I would have done without the priest."

"The priest! These people tell you what you want to know. That's all they do. Here we are sitting in this room and we are all hiding things aren't we? Our good host is hiding the fact that he doesn't like me. You're hiding the fact that you don't like me. And your good mother, Mr Mallow, is hiding the fact that she doesn't like me either. And we are all religious people. Yet I'm sure . . ." she stopped suddenly, gazing at them in a sort of drunken astonishment. "I see it all. Beyond language, beyond good manners, beyond society, beyond all that, we hate each other. Oh I know you think I'm drunk but I'm not drunk. I'm just telling the truth and nobody likes to hear the truth. Why doesn't Mr Mallow like me? Tell me that. Well, I'll tell you then. It's because he doesn't like people who tell him the truth. Perhaps he doesn't like his mother to be unhappy. Perhaps that's why he brought her here. Perhaps he doesn't even like her. Tell me that, Mr Mallow."

"Look, Miss Donaldson," said Tom fixing her with enraged eyes, "we're putting up with a lot from you. You seem to be confusing argument with bad manners. However if you're putting us in the situation that you want the truth since that seems to be your gimmick for tonight, I'll tell you something. It's none of your business but I brought my mother here because that is what one ought to do."

"Why?"

"Why? Because I want to look after her."

"Do you really?"

The words hung between them for a long moment like a challenging flag above a battlefield and then Ruth Donaldson said, "I'm sorry. I shouldn't have said that. Perhaps I should leave."

"No," said Tom decisively for at that moment he was struck by pity for her unhappiness and recognising that the pity was nevertheless a weakness, he repeated, "No. There is no reason why the truth should not be spoken when the truth is necessary, and I suppose it's always necessary."

"It's all right, Miss Donaldson," said his mother. "It's all right. Don't worry about me."

Tom looked from one to the other and his pity was for the two of them, for their stricken faces, for the terror that haunted the table, and he thought: I'm the liberal, the useless liberal. I am being tormented by too much pity and reason. I should be harder than I am. If I weren't weak I should put this woman out of the house beyond the circle of our welcome, into the darkness to howl like a wolf there if she wants to. If I had any deep feeling that's what I should do, if I had principles. But all he did was to say to Vera, "I'll help you to bring the sweet in." And he got up from the table followed by Vera. Finding himself alone with her he shut the door fiercely behind him,

"I hope you're satisfied. What the hell are you up to?" He went up to her and thrust his face against hers.

"What do you mean what am I up to?"

"I told you not to bring that woman here, and now look what's happening. She's creating hell in there just because she's unhappy."

"And what about me?" Vera retorted equally fiercely, "Do you not think that I'm unhappy?"

"You? What are you unhappy about?"

"What am I unhappy about? I see you going back more and more to your mother and leaving me behind and you ask me what I'm unhappy about."

"What are you talking about?" said Tom in genuine astonishment.

"Oh, perhaps you don't see it. But I see it. You went to church with her, you betrayed your principles, and what did you do that for except that you love her more than you love me."

The rain and wind could be heard beating strongly against the window and in the middle of the roar and the torrent, but protected for the moment against it, the two of them stood staring at each other, the plates forgotten on the table.

"What do you mean I love my mother more than I love you? I thought you said that reason was enough. If we were reasonable, you said."

"I know I said that but I was wrong. Reason has nothing to do with it. I can't help it if I see you leaving me day after day. You want to be with her."

"I don't understand you. I love my mother but that has nothing to do with my love for you."

As he looked at her it seemed to him that her marble poise, her glacial whiteness, were beginning to melt in front of his eyes.

"What's wrong with you?" he asked making as if to touch her.

"Keep away from me. It never occurred to you that I've been suffering though you're very concerned about your mother's sufferings. All your principles are for others not for me."

"Oh to hell," said Tom banging the table with his fist in frustration, "one tries one's best and then everything is spoiled by people's ridiculous emotions. By trivialities."

"There you go again. Trivialities. Anything that's serious you call a triviality. It's not a triviality. It's life."

"What did you say?"

"I said it's life, something you've never thought about and never understood. Life. That's the word I used."

And then Tom felt a dreadful sorrow descending on him like a frightening disease, a sorrow worse than he had ever known. Life, was this then life, this conflict. Was life after all choice? Up until that moment he had never had to make a real choice, he had been protected by words and badinage, by the smooth progression of his days. Was this then really life, this shell of a lighted room beaten upon by the wind and the rain, the two of them as if afloat in a gale, on the stormy bitter waters?

They gazed at each other like enemies across the table on which lay the plates and the spoons and the glittering knives.

"We'll talk about it later," he said.

"We've talked about it long enough. You want to go home to your mother. Can you not see that in inviting her here that is exactly what you were doing? You were avoiding death. You were avoiding old age. You thought you would keep her alive forever. Is that not what you thought?"

"No," he shouted in agony, "No."

"Yes, yes, yes," she said but more quietly than him, "Yes, it is what you were doing. You wanted perfection, you wanted to be her child again. And now if you'll kindly get out of my way, I'll take the sweet in." He followed her into the room where the three women were sitting in a tense silence and helped her to put the plates on the table.

They ate their sweets without incident and then returned to the living room and sat down in their chairs again leaving the dishes to be washed later. Vera poured out more drinks for everyone except Mrs Mallow.

From then on, Tom, drinking heavily, felt the evening becoming more and more unreal as if by allowing Ruth Donaldson her bridge-head he had made an almost complete surrender.

At one point in the evening, Mrs Murphy suggested a sing song, and the two of them accompanied occasionally by his mother sang 'Danny Boy' while Vera gazed at them disapprovingly. But Tom had given up thinking and he sang the verses of the song as if he were descending with Mrs Murphy to a world forever lost yet forever, humiliatingly, yearned for.

> The summer's gone and now the leaves are falling,
> Tis you, tis you, must go, and I must bide.

Through a haze of cigarette smoke and drink, he saw the exiled Mrs Murphy reaching back into her sentimental past, as if to drink at these false waters, and he was with her, dancing in the middle of the floor, and watching his wife and Ruth Donaldson, stony-faced, regarding them. But he didn't care. Out of his mouth and out of his heart poured that momently-loved music, while beside him on the sofa, splay-legged and happily prominent, there sat Mrs Murphy, who had bowed to her audience after the song. Pal of mine, he thought, salt of the earth, ould Mrs Murphy friend of my youth, representative of healthy humanity, dance for us again, fertility symbol, honest staircleaner in our waste land, leprechaun of green old emerald Ireland.

And drunkenly he turned to Ruth Donaldson, "What did you think of that eh? Where thou goest I shall go, eh? I saw you looking at my wife," and he wagged his finger playfully at her, "Oh I saw you, religious expert. Let's have some truth now. Let's have some truth. And the truth is this. Why do you hate every honest emotion? Are you visiting the sins of the mothers on us, eh? But the truth is, dear Ruth, that we've failed. We've all failed. You've failed and we've all failed. We've all failed to be human beings. Haven't you in particular, if I may speak in my gauche way, failed to understand, haven't you? It's all very simple really. Everything is very simple. Haven't you failed to understand?"

"I have failed to understand nothing. Mr Mallow. It is you who have failed to understand."

"Not at all, dear Ruth, not at all. On the contrary, if I may be so bold as to say so, on the contrary. Here we have Mrs Murphy, Irish Catholic, and a good singer and member of the human race. She gives, Miss Donaldson, she gives. And you. What do you give? Nothing. That's the difference. She is alive, dear Ruth, and you, dear Ruth, are dead. Listen to the wind and the rain. Do you hear it? The storm. Into the storm we all go, some more happily than others. More humanly. I speak the truth in wine, I am the Dostoyevskyan fool. And you are the cold idiot. You know nothing and you understand nothing and you drag your unhappiness with you like an old skirt, and you impose it on others. That's all you do, dear Ruth. Come on speak the truth. Or would you prefer to dance?"

He got to his feet and linking arms with his mother and Mrs Murphy waltzed them about the room, and then sank down on the sofa again.

"That's right," said Mrs Murphy her eyes glancing mischievously. "In Ireland we would give you the bread from our lips. We would bring you the water from the well. We would bring you the peat for the fire. And we would bring you the song for your throat."

"Did you hear that," said Tom excitedly, "did you hear that, mavourneen?"

"And now," he said, getting unsteadily to his feet, "I am about to take Mrs Murphy home. I'm going to run Mrs Murphy home and I'm going to leave you here, Miss Donaldson, for a while."

Staggering about the room he managed to get Mrs Murphy her fur coat and led her to the car past the bathroom whose door was open and in which there sat the staring doll with the intense blue eyes.

In her bowlegged duck-like way, Mrs Murphy scuttled through the wind and rain towards the car whose door he opened quickly and then drove off erratically among the many lights till he had deposited her at her door. In a sudden quietness he said, "I hope you enjoyed your evening, Mrs Murphy."

"Fine, Mr Mallow, just fine," she said, and then she was out of the car and in the close, and he waved to her as she turned round once only, and he knew that she probably would never be in his house again. So he waved once more, slightly drunkenly, and turned the car in a whirl of spray towards the house. Arriving, he opened the door of the car, and after springing through the rain and wind and entering the living room he saw only the two women there, his mother having gone, Ruth Donaldson's head bent towards his wife's white dress, as the two of them half sat half lay on the sofa beside the table which was littered with bottles and glasses.

He rushed over to Ruth Donaldson, dragged her away, and pushed her from his wife who gazed up at him with a triumphant face. He rushed Ruth Donaldson along the hall and out the door into the wind and rain, banging it solidly behind her, and then walked slowly back to the living room. In a sudden access of what might have been rage or despair or desire he thrust himself on top of his wife, pulling viciously at her dress till he had got it up and over her knees. In a brutal silence they fought for mastery, he bending his mouth over hers like a beak, the two of them fighting all over the sofa in a pulsating gasping combat, till he had finally pinned her to the floor to which they had rolled, forgetful even that his mother might come in, and entered her as she suddenly quietened, as she put her arms around his neck, as she pulled him down on top of her, and they came together in a fiercer communion than they had ever known.

2

WHEN TOM ROSE the following morning (which was a Saturday) he left Vera still in bed, curled up almost in a foetal position under the bedclothes. His head heavy and sore he wandered into the living room where the curtains were still drawn, the table in the ghostly twilight crowded with glasses, and the cupboard whose door was open revealing the bottles of whisky and wine. He pulled the curtains aside, and looked out on a ravaged landscape, branches and leaves strewn on the ground in front of the house, pools of water glinting in a pale sun. He tidied the room and went into the kitchen where the plates and cutlery remained unwashed. He washed and dried them and then went into the bathroom to shave. The razor shook in his hand, his face, white and strained, seeming to repeat the appearance of the distraught landscape outside. Moon man, he thought, where is your Fisher King, shall you at least set your lands in order, this tumbler here, that soap there, that doll with the staring blue eyes in the other place, a constellation of trivia. Here in the mirror is my face, perturbed, lunar, shaken by its troubles. I have tidied my world till it is untidied again, till the next storm comes. With grim satisfaction he recalled the limping Miss Donaldson setting off into the night, while the branches plucked at her hair, and her warlock face (for he thought of her as half masculine) shook among the changing pools of water.

As he walked back to the living room he heard sounds from his mother's room and knocked on the door. When he entered she was bent over a case.

"What are you doing?"

"I'm packing," she replied standing up and looking at him. In the mirror he could see her face, wrinkled and old.

"Listen," he said, his voice trembling, "you can't do that. In any case there is no place to go. Let's talk this over."

"There is nothing to talk over," she said stubbornly. "I shall have to go."

"NO," he heard himself shouting. "NO."

"I have to go," she repeated in a tired voice. "No one wants me here," and her voice was whining and dull. "You know that."

"You can't go," he said. "So you had better put all that back," and in spite of himself he stared into the case noticing how old the clothes were, how much older than his wife's silky ones. My heart is breaking, he thought, I can't take any more of this, I have too much pity. I can't be continually seeing people coming and going as if they were leaving on trains, I should have let things remain as they were from the beginning. I have made a mistake, I should never have brought her here at all. I should have thought less about principles, more about life.

"I don't blame you," said his mother quietly. "It's not your fault. Don't think I blame you." But you blame me just the same, yes you blame me. How could you not? Is this another part of the drama, this setting out into the watery landscape towards the station, the rails, which my father once haunted. He is waiting for her there, silent, reproachful, in his cheap uniform as if directing her into the last station. There is a cloud of steam and he is standing in the middle of it, tiny, pitiful.

His mother's whining voice grated through the room, "You've got your own life. It's not my life. You've got your career. I don't fit in here."

My career. Straight as rails, climbing, climbing, leaving my father and mother there below, panting, distant, small. My career diminished and faded.

"You're like your father. You want to keep the peace at all costs. That's what you're doing. He was the same. I often used to say to him, 'Why don't you stand up for yourself?' But he wouldn't. He didn't want to cause trouble. And what did he get from them at the end. Nothing. You're just like him."

I have to deal with you also, I have to understand you too, and I'm so tired, so desperately tired. So much pain in the world, so much understanding required, and I don't have enough. Everyone has his own world, his antennae, crying, listen to me, pay attention to me, you are ignoring me.

"I know you wanted to help," she said in the same whining voice. "I know that. I'm not blaming you." They looked at each other across the ravaged landscape.

"You can't go away today anyway," he said. "The train will have gone by now."

Not today. Give me time. I'll work something out. Didn't you know I was Mr Micawber, didn't you know that?

"I never liked her anyway," said his mother and he gazed at her as if he didn't understand what she was talking about.

"Who?"

"Your wife. I never liked her. From the day I met her. She's not your kind. She's not our kind."

What is she talking about? This mirror, what is it telling me, these two actors opening their mouths and speaking, what are they saying?

"I don't understand her. She comes from a different background. She doesn't understand."

"Mother, she is my wife."

"I know. Your father and I got on so well. Always." And yet at the back of his mind were those other nights, days, when they hadn't got on so well, when she had said to him, I'm tired of this flat, this slum, when are we going to get a new house, there's no place to hang out clothes, the close is so dirty. Out of the tenement the voices came back to him with the pathos of early days, irrevocable, finished. What had he been thinking of? What had she been thinking of? What lies had they told each other?

"Leave it," he pleaded, "for a while." You can't go out into the storm, not with that case, not with your hat on askew, not talking to trains in dead tenements.

She remained for a moment bent over her case and then said, "I'd thought you would have got some other wife, someone more like ourselves. Someone more ordinary." And the pang went through him, a very fine intent needle. "I never told you before. You never came back much, did you? Not after you left. And yet I remember the days when we were so close, when I used to knit your socks for you."

I remember, I remember. The laburnum among the tenements. Close against the sky. She is sly, she is pleading with me, by indirections, obliquely. Using old quotations. We are all alone, we are all using every weapon we have, every single armament.

113

How did I not know this before, how could I have been so ignorant and naïve?

"Even the day of your wedding. I wasn't in the photograph, it was that father and mother of hers. You didn't even have a proper wedding. Not that I don't like the father, but I can't stand the mother, I never could."

She sat on the bed in a pose reminiscent of someone he had once seen. What now was she demanding of him as she had demanded of him in the past? Remember I am not well, so don't stay up late, your father has to go to his work in the morning.

"Remember," she was saying, "that Mrs Murphy will spread this round. She looks harmless enough but do you think she won't? All these people in the tenements are the same, you should know that. She'll be telling them all about it, and you've got a position to keep up. You were always the same, taking people at their face value. She's a gossip like everybody else and don't you think different. And what about that Miss Donaldson? What is she going to say in the school? You don't think of things like that."

She stopped putting her things in the case and was speaking fluently and easily. "Everyone thinks I don't know anything. Oh I can see it right enough, I can see what's happening right enough. You disgraced yourself with that Mrs Murphy singing songs with her. What is she going to think of you? What respect will she give you, tell me that. There was an Irishwoman just like her in the tenement where we lived, a big fat woman who was always gossiping. She would say to people that I wasn't doing the stairs right, that I should put pipeclay on them. Oh, don't tell me about them, I know their kind. All they want is something to talk about, and they're so nice to your face too."

Don't leave me, mother, not yet. I know you will have to leave but not yet. It's not that I don't see you for what you are, it's not that I didn't see you as you are, it's something else. I'm bleeding for myself, that I can't secure you, mean-minded as you are, as we all are, against the ravages of time, perfect, silent. It is for myself that I am weeping bitterly, it is for a whole world, that we aren't better than we are, that we are so inconsistent, petty, lacking all nobility. It was not your loneliness that I was concerned with, it was my own.

114

"Leave it for a day or two at least," he said. "Just for a day or two. Surely that won't do any harm. Put your case away. Just for a day or two. Something might happen."

Something might turn up. In all reasonableness. He put the case under the bed.

Child, even though you are old don't run away from home as a child might do. Let us part in peace, at least in peace.

"I'll go and make the breakfast," he said, "Vera isn't up yet. I'll make the breakfast. Don't do anything foolish. Promise me. Promise me that. Will you promise me that?" Child, pupil, will you promise?

"All right, Tom," she said, "all right."

He left the room and went to make the breakfast though he didn't feel like eating. Still one had to eat for that was what kept one alive. Salvation was in routine, not in the storms: in rings, in rails, in the tables that have to be cleared, the beds that have to be made, the food that has to be cooked. If it were not so someone would have told us. Some priest, some minister, someone.

PART THREE

1

IT WAS TWO or three weeks later, on a particularly fine day in autumn, intensely still and clear, as if the year were pausing for a moment before proceeding to its decline: considering, taking the measure of its success or failure: that Vera's mother, Angela, erupted from her small red car in front of their house, having driven impulsively from Edinburgh.

"My dear," she said to Vera as she removed her fur and coat, "Would you and Tom please get my cases out of my car, there's a good girl. I'm staying for two or three days. I haven't decided yet. Your father couldn't drag himself away from his codicils and torts so I had this wonderful idea of driving up to see you. You should see Loch Lomond, absolutely still, exactly like a mirror, I mean exactly. You're looking pale. Is there anything wrong. And Tom. You're looking pale too. Is the daily grind getting too much for you? Thank God I got out of the rat race when I married your father thirty years ago though it seems considerably longer. And Chrissie too. How are you?" And she kissed Mrs Mallow with a flourish.

It seemed for a moment as if the house had been turned into a theatre, as if lights had been turned up, as if a spotlight focussed itself on her as she continued to talk, the others listening.

"Your father, Vera," she burbled, "couldn't or wouldn't come. He said to me or rather grunted, 'If you wish to go just go but at least you should phone to say you're coming.' Well, my dear, I didn't take his advice in that or anything else. And here I am. I thought I would descend on you in my little car and my red coat (don't you think they match rather well?) almost like a female Father Christmas (if that isn't a mixed metaphor or something, Tom) which we might soon have, Women's Lib being what it is. In any case I left him there buried in papers, contorted in his torts, graved in his affidavits, and set off into the glorious morning. Edinburgh, my dear, is beautiful just now but so is your little town. And the Festival is finished. Do you know I saw six plays, half of them about Russian uncles and aunts (Chekhov has much to answer for), listened to four concerts and had a small tug at the Fringe, most of it very amateurish, I'm sorry to say. Aren't you going to give me a coffee, Vera, after coming all this way? I hope someone will talk to me, you're all looking so glum. Is anything the matter? And how are you settling down, Chrissie, among the grammarians? Have you enough to do? I'm sure Tom and Vera are so busy marking the exercises of our next illiterate generation that they have little time for the social niceties. How are they doing, our new drug-taking elite, Tom? But of course you don't think of them like that, do you? You're probably saying to yourself, 'Who's she to talk?' and you're quite right too. Who indeed am I? Who indeed is anyone?"

"They are doing as well as can be expected," said Tom laughingly as if he were delivering a medical bulletin.

"Good, good. For a moment there I was afraid that you had lost your sense of humour. Ah, here's Vera with the coffee. My daughter has learned to make good coffee. At one time I thought I would never get her head out of a book and dreaming of being an orphan in darkest Yorkshire—or was it Belgium?—and now she's treating her aged mother. Did I ever tell you, Tom and Chrissie, that my own parents were dull people, even duller than Jeff and me. That is probably why I decided to become flamboyant, and don't say that I'm not for I should never forgive you. My father and mother were the sort of people (or should I say sorts, Tom?) who never said boo to a goose, not even the most harmless of them, who hid from the world going past them especially when it threw splashes of water on them like one used to get from the buses before one grew affluent and never walked anywhere any more. My Father was a dull lawyer just like dear Jeff whom I love in spite of his addiction to torts (how like a disease the word sounds, some very decisive disease, some malady of the bones at any rate). This coffee is quite good, Vera, quite passable. In any case, that's why I became flamboyant. I wasn't going to let the world pass me by. I meant to make it sit up and listen. You've heard me talking of my father and mother, haven't you, Vera? Your grandfather was the kind of man who, if he noticed children at all, would tell the housekeeper to take them away as if they were to be put on a shovel somewhere. In any case I became theatrical and Vera became bookish. It's a great mistake however to let life pass one by, isn't it, Tom?"

"I suppose so," said Tom, "though it depends on what you mean by life."

"There you go again speaking like dear Jeff and that man who used to be on the Brains Trust, though for the moment I can't recall his name, some professor was it. Toad? No surely it couldn't have been that though it doesn't really matter." She gazed piercingly at them, her eyes sparkling with a keen intelligence, and it seemed to them, even to Vera, that she had descended from a larger world which diminished their own, that she had blown fresh air on to a structure which had become slightly self-regarding and mirror-like, that she was in short making them feel uncomfortable.

"Anyway," she said, "I think you two should go and wash the coffee cups and do whatever else you have to do, and leave me and Chrissie together for a while. We two old people have our own concerns," and again her eyes flashed disconcertingly with that sudden sharp light.

When the two had left, she turned to Mrs Mallow and said, "And how are you, my dear?"

"Oh I'm fine, fine," said Mrs Mallow. Overwhelmed by this strange bird of vivid plumage, articulate and knowledgeable and continually in motion, she found it very difficult to say anything much to her, and only felt envy that she couldn't be like her.

"Your son is a good boy, Chrissie. And Vera? Vera is an odd girl. You see, Chrissie, I've always believed in letting people alone. Maybe I've left Vera too much alone. Do you think she likes me?"

"I'm sure," Mrs Mallow began nervously.

"Oh, but I'm not, Chrissie, I'm not at all sure, Vera is very self-contained. Still waters run deep as the proverb says, and too many cooks spoil the broth is another old saw. No, Chrissie, I'm not at all sure about Vera, she's always been a girl who liked being on her own. I, on the other hand, am not like that. I prefer people to isolation. The world is so full of riches. Do you know that the other day I was talking to a tramp who came to the door. He told me he spent his nights sleeping among the haystacks. There's a bit of the gipsy in me: I should like to wear a kaftan and wander about the world. But the two of them love each other, I know that. They're so alike you see, in so many ways, except that Vera is harder. Tom is too soft for his own good, and he keeps tripping over his ideals all the time. They remind me of two children in a fairy story, they don't know anything of the world. And we have to accept reality at the end, don't we, Chrissie?" And again she turned her piercing disconcerting gaze on Mrs Mallow. "Don't you believe that?"

For perhaps the first time in her life in her dealings with Angela, Mrs Mallow found some words to speak. "I think," she said slowly and carefully, as if she were measuring out her words, "that you can't tell. I think that your life is so different from mine that you can't understand. That's what I think, though I know that you mean well." And then she was abruptly silent as if there was nothing more that she wished to say.

"That's true, I suppose, in a way," said Angela not at all offended but as if she were giving the matter her undivided attention. "I don't really know. And yet . . . I suppose that you think my life with Jeff has been some sort of idyll. Well I can assure you that that is not the case. There are times when I could scream when I see him sitting there in his chair just as self-contained as his daughter. There are times when I feel I could walk out of there and take a long journey somewhere, anywhere. You see, people like Jeff and Vera," she considered them objectively as if they were strangers, "are so self-centred it isn't true. My husband deals with the law but he doesn't know anything of the pains of living, nothing at all. Neither does Vera. They are incapable of sympathy, they cannot put themselves in the position of anyone else. It's a fact of life that the rest of us have to endure as best we can. I remember one night when I was sitting in the room with Jeff and I was going over old photographs while he was reading the *Scotsman* I came on our wedding photograph. For some reason I burst out crying, and Jeff put the *Scotsman* down and looked at me over his glasses and said, 'What on earth is wrong with you?' He was incapable of understanding the tears of things, you see. And for that moment I hated him, because of his perfect inability to feel anything, a trait of his," she added absently, "I rely a great deal on in the affairs of daily life." She stopped, and said, "Anyway I've been speaking too much. Perhaps we should go and see what the two young ones are doing."

For the rest of that day, while Angela moved theatrically about the house, Mrs Mallow felt not only the inferiority of a mind much slower than that of Angela's but also, which was more surprising, a certain ease and relief, for Angela was drawing attention away from her, leaving her in a considering silence of her own. It seemed to her that Angela was essentially an unhappy woman and this in spite of the fact that her husband was still alive, and that in much the same way as she herself didn't communicate with Vera, so Angela was finding difficulty in that direction as well. It wasn't so much that anything was actually said to reveal the antagonism between the two women, but rather as if the unease and awkwardness hung in the air between them. It was as if Mrs Mallow realised, after a long period of silence during which she had idealised her former circumstances, that antagonism and discomfort were the normal relationships in a house where more than one person lived: and she remembered, as it were unwillingly, days and nights when she had quarrelled with her own husband or with Tom.

So this, after all, is life, she thought, this antagonism, and without it there is no life. And yet she also thought, I want peace, I want to be away from it all. She sometimes gazed at the unhappy face of her son when he wasn't looking at her, and thought, He is no longer mine, he has to make his own way in the world, and this is the world in which he will have to live. When he was growing up he was sometimes difficult and rebellious, now he is embroiled in the battle for daily living. How little I really know about him, she thought.

"I wonder," she said aloud, "I wonder what happened to that Miss Donaldson. Have you seen her since?" she asked Vera.

"I haven't been speaking to her," said Vera. "I have seen her from a distance."

"Of course," said Mrs Mallow.

And Tom looked at the two of them as if he was wondering whether they shared a secret.

It seemed at that moment that Vera was about to say something when her mother interrupted her to ask who Miss Donaldson was and Tom explained to her, though he didn't mention the party which had been so disastrous.

But after all, Ruth Donaldson, Mrs Mallow thought, had created her own unhappiness, had allowed it to overwhelm her, had, in her unexamined simplicity, turned against the world, and if you turned against the world then the world turned against you. The world wasn't interested in those who, hating it, turned their back on it, for the world could afford to dispense with these people. Ruth Donaldson was like a log which the tide had washed on to the shore but which was too far away now for the full tide to reach it and then float it out again.

It was funny, thought Mrs Mallow, how secretively Vera had smiled when they had mentioned Miss Donaldson, as if there were something she knew that none of them knew, as yet. It had been a small triumphant smile turned first on Tom and then on her mother and finally on her, Mrs Mallow.

While Angela in full spate was discussing a play by Chekhov which according to her was about some sisters who had wanted to go to Moscow but had never done so ("Didn't they have trains in those days?" she asked) Mrs Mallow was thinking about Ruth Donaldson and her unhappiness. It was as if the large ugly limping woman represented some sort of a sign to her, as if she were trying to give her a message, though she couldn't think what the message was.

Halfway through the meal, Angela excused herself to go to the bathroom and when she came back said to Vera, "I see that you've still got that doll there, the one with the blue eyes."

"Yes," said Vera non-committally.

Angela didn't pursue the subject but continued with her food.

I can't understand women, Tom thought, here they are all around me, creating webs of words and hidden emotions, and I feel as if I don't belong here, not to them. If only . . . He imagined himself under a tree in a wood on an autumn day with a bottle of wine in his hand, drinking slowly and chastely, while a squirrel flashed in and out among the dappled lights and shadows of the tree trunk. They are different from me, he thought, and then: My mother must go, but I wish that she should go only after learning first why she should. In life, he asked himself, is there no catharsis after all? Or is it only an untidiness that has no frontier, no end?

"I think," he said, "that I shall go and make a start on the garden. Get rid of some of the boulders."

Vera looked at him with a triumphant secretive smile as if she knew something that he didn't know; but in fact all he wanted to do was to hold a solid implement in his hand, a direct unchanging spade.

"Yes," said Angela, "that will do you good. What should we do without our gardens?"

Mrs Mallow felt all sorts of uncomprehended words floating all round her, a secret unplumbable language, all the more so when Vera remarked, "Yes, we've been very neglectful."

Mrs Mallow herself loved her garden and there was nothing she liked better than to sit there in the summer evenings when the roses hung white and fragile from their stems and somewhere in the distance faint and almost scented the pale moon climbed into the sky, as if it were a reminder of the past.

"I have had a letter from the people I rented my house to," she told Angela.

"Oh?"

"They have a baby and he's a chartered accountant. The letter was very nice. I think they will look after my house all right."

"I'm sure," said Angela. "They are probably very responsible people."

"Yes, I think so."

But at that moment Mrs Mallow had an intense desire for her house, as sharp as hunger or thirst, a desire to sit by herself in it so that she would not have to speak to anyone, but simply relax there, in an undemanding silence, which might of course later turn to a demanding one.

She looked out of the window at Tom who was leaning over his spade among the uncultivated ground. He seemed to be miles away. And so did Angela and Vera.

"I think," she said, "I shall go to my room for a little while, and lie down. Oh I'm all right, there's nothing wrong with me, I am just tired."

Her last glimpse was of the two women, Vera and her mother, sitting opposite each other at the table, not speaking, while in the garden outside Tom was digging furiously with his spade.

2

IN HER DREAM Mrs Mallow was shouting at her husband, "Why can't you get a better job than working on the railway? We never have any money. We have nothing." And she stared fiercely at her old black kitchen range, at the linoleum instead of a carpet on the floor, at the sink discoloured and veined. "We have nothing at all," she screamed. "And that son of yours," she shouted, "what's he going to do? He sits here all day after school and he doesn't speak to anyone. What sort of person is he?"

She stared out at the backs of the houses, at the washing hung from the windows, at the blank grey yard. If only we had a garden, she thought, if only . . .

I wish I could stop this shouting she was saying to herself over and over, but she couldn't.

What? What did the doctor say to you?

And he stood there in front of her like a schoolboy, and he wasn't at all frightened, only resigned, as if he had arrived at a terminus which he had been driving towards all his life. No, she said, that can't be right. You must see another doctor. He must be lying. I will go with you.

And they set off through the streets of Edinburgh together on that brisk fine breezy spring day. No, she was repeating to herself let it not happen. Not . . . not . . . not . . . It can't be true. I loved you, I love you.

The insurance, he was saying something about the insurance. Something about the insurance and a garden. What was he talking about, an insurance and a garden. What was the connection? But he was going on about it in such an unhurried even voice almost as if he were talking about someone else. His body would be converted to a garden, he would flourish there. He would grow out of the garden, his buried body would blossom. And she clutched his hand. My love, my useless love, only your death, you are saying, will bring me my garden. No, no, no, there had been the two of them, there were the two of them, and of course Tom. And her mother and father hadn't come to see her much, neither had his parents. They had been dependent on each other, and now he was talking about insurance. Death was something that happened to other people, not to her, especially on such a fine sparkling day as this. It couldn't happen, there was no sense to it. Yes she could have lived forever in that tenement, put up with anything, if only he had been there with her. Perhaps with her nagging she had . . . Her mind winced away from the unbearable thought. They crossed the park, and the squirrels were playing games among the tree trunks, in the deft interplay of light and shadow, and there was a child playing with a red ball. The doctor would tell her that it had been a mistake, surely he would. But then if he didn't . . . And her husband never went to church, though she did. He stopped for a moment and stood under a tree looking up at the pale white blossoms and then continued on his way, she beside him. Just for a while there he had stopped as if he had seen something. Soon she would know.

"The insurance," he said again.

And for the first time she really thought about the insurance and the house and garden it might buy her. It seemed to her that she screamed like a train in the night.

3

THE FOLLOWING MORNING Mrs Mallow and Angela went for a walk down to the town. As they strolled along the street, Angela would say now and again, "I see the butcher's has been changed to a jeweller's and the draper's to a confectionery shop. That, I suppose, is what one calls life." Once she stopped and remarked, "I think if I were living in a small town like this I would know everybody and as I grew older I would meet, wheeling a pram, a little girl whom I had once known. The mortality of it would be too much for me. At least we are spared that in the city." It seemed to annoy her that so many of the shops had changed hands, that while she had been away the town had continued its own distant life, that without her it had survived and prospered and altered.

"I remember," she said, "that when I was here last I used to buy my newspapers at what is now that restaurant. I don't like it at all. Not at all. Still, you have always got the sea. That at least doesn't change."

Mrs Murphy was waiting on her bench as usual when Mrs Mallow arrived at the small garden with Angela, and she introduced the two of them. All three then sat on the bench among the late autumn flowers.

"And which part of Ireland do you come from, Mrs Murphy?" Angela asked. "I have been to Ireland with my husband. It's a very pretty part of the world. I used to see donkeys drawing carts, and there were a number of nuns. There was also much gorse and many stones."

"I come from Connemara myself," said Mrs Murphy, "though I don't go back there now."

"And why don't you go back there? Is it because you grew tired of it?"

"Not at all. I have no relatives there now. The family is all dead."

"Well, that is a good reason, I suppose. And do you like living here?"

"At times I do and at times I don't," said Mrs Murphy, "but

we have to put up with things, and that is all there is to it."

"Of course that is true," said Angela glancing restlessly around her. "I myself was not born in Edinburgh though I live there now. It is very true what you have just said, that we have to put up with things. What did you use to work at?"

"I used to clean stairs," said Mrs Murphy firmly.

"Now isn't that interesting," said Angela to Mrs Mallow. "It's my experience that if you ever meet a woman on a train she has been doing something uninteresting like teaching. But to clean stairs. I'm sure you must have found that fascinating. You must have met such a lot of different people. It's the sort of job that I myself would have liked to do if I had had the courage. It's a useful job, far more useful in my experience than teaching. Tell me, do you have any sons or daughters?"

"Yes, but I live alone now."

"Alone?" and Angela glanced briefly at Mrs Mallow.

"I can do what I like any time that I like," said Mrs Murphy.

"That is one way of looking at it," Angela mused absently, and then suddenly, "what is it like then to live alone? Do you never fear death?"

"Death?" Mrs Murphy echoed as if she had never heard of the word before. "I never think about it, to tell you the truth. I get up in the morning and I have my breakfast and I wash and dry the dishes. Then I come out here into God's good air and I look around me a bit and I fill my lungs. Then in the evening I watch the television. In the mornings I go to Mass. I don't think about death. Not at all."

"You are a very brave woman. Isn't she a brave woman?" she asked Mrs Mallow. The latter was so embarrassed that she couldn't think of anything to say.

"I think that that is what I would fear the most," Angela meditated. "That is, if I were living alone. I admire you a great deal."

"There is nothing to admire," Mrs Murphy replied.

"Oh, but there is. To remain cheerful as you so obviously do when you are living alone. That is heroic. Many have been called heroes for less." He red cloak glittered in the autumnal day, a shield among the fading flowers.

129

"I wish I had your courage. To live from day to day. That is the important thing. So few of us are able to do that. We plan ahead and then the plans turn to dust and ashes in our mouths. But to live from day to day, that is the heroic thing. That is the thing. However it is possible that that is not the whole story. Is it the whole story?"

Mrs Murphy looked at her with a new interest as if she had sensed behind the bird of plumage a common and ordinary strength. Then she smiled for the first time,

"You are thinking," she said slowly, "that it is lying I am."

"No, no, nothing as drastic as that, not at all. I was merely suggesting that perhaps you are showing us your public self, that part of you which as you say is making the best of things. Perhaps you are simply telling us now that you are not afraid of death in this sunshine. Perhaps you are making yourself out to be slightly better than you are in that respect. I have had much experience of people. For instance there was a guru who seemed to me to be very strong and firm but he turned out to be a secret alcoholic. Not of course that I am suggesting that you are. Not at all. But there must be a weakness somewhere in all of us, and in those who live alone as much as in those who don't."

As if she had issued a challenge she waited with great interest for the answer.

Mrs Murphy still smiling said, "I know what you are saying. You don't have to explain it to me. I will tell you the truth and no lying. When you have to do something you have to do it and that is all there is to it. Many people I know have lived alone and some of them have gone off their heads. Some of them have taken to the bottle and some of them are hearing voices, would you believe it? There was a woman I used to know once. She lived on her own and after a while she used to think that everybody was talking about her. When they waved their arms when they were talking that was how she used to know. Well one day she saw a policeman directing the traffic and she went up to him and gave him a piece of her mind because she thought he was taking the mickey out of her. I remember her well. In every other way, you understand, she was right as rain. She was frightened, you see."

"And are you not frightened?" Angela asked eagerly.

"I can't afford to be. If I feel frightened I go and clean a room. That is what I do."

"So admirable," said Angela to Mrs Mallow, "so admirable. You are a very fortunate woman."

She seemed lost in reverie for a while and then she said, "There are so many different kinds of people in the world. Mrs Mallow is fortunate to have you as her friend." And then as if unwilling to give up,

"Do you never find the time heavy on your hands?"

"Sometimes. Not often."

"Ah, well You are all armour. You are all armour. I retire defeated. May I treat you both to a cup of coffee?"

"I wouldn't say no to that," said Mrs Murphy and together they entered a restaurant which was crowded with people, mostly women, who were in for their morning coffee.

Suddenly Mrs Murphy said to Mrs Mallow, "There's one thing I forgot to tell you. I saw that girl Ruth Donaldson recently."

"Oh?"

"She came up to me in the street. She apologised to me. She told me she hadn't been feeling well. As a matter of fact, I think she has had a hard life of it." And a strange almost triumphant smile crossed her face briefly.

"Maybe we shouldn't judge her too hard. I took her to the house and gave her tea. She is a very miserable woman, that one. She made one mistake," and she paused.

"And what mistake was that?" said Angela.

"She blamed the world for what happened to her. That's no good. The world won't take the blame for things like that. It's like the land in Connemara. If you blame the Lord for the big stones you won't do anything at all. I told her she should go to Mass but she wouldn't. She's a clever girl but she's not a clever girl at all if you see what I mean. I knew what she was up to right enough," she said to Mrs Mallow. "Oh, I could see right enough. But I'm not going to say any more."

Angela glanced from one woman to another, not understanding what they were talking about but sensing its significance. She stirred her coffee with her plastic spoon.

"Oh I knew right enough," said Mrs. Murphy again, "but she apologised. I said she could come back any time she liked. She's a very unhappy woman. Maybe she would have been better cleaning stairs," she added and burst out laughing so that the coffee cup shook in her hand.

There are those, thought Angela looking at her, who are strong, and there are the others who are weak. For instance, she thought that she herself was weak and so perhaps was Mrs Mallow. Unlike Mrs Murphy they had not as yet recognised the necessity and inevitability of things. It was so simple if one could grasp it: all one had to do was to go with the current, be a part of the day like a stone or a tree. But something in her said, No, that is not enough: we would not then be men or women, we would be only stones. We must flash for a little while, we must spark, send out flames. We must create the theatre of the imagination.

And it seemed to her that as Mrs Murphy shook with laughter, the tiny cup in her hand, she was like an old wrinkled Celtic goddess, who had about her the reality and clay of the earth, secretive, yet public, strong and peasant-like, yet in the end lacking in fineness, in a necessary fineness. She imagined her on her hands and knees climbing stair after stair but the stone was all that was in front of her eyes. What door had opened to her or would open to her at the top of the stair? What illuminating door?

"I think," she said, "that Mrs Mallow and I must be going now. We have to make our lunch." Mrs Mallow glanced at her in surprise but stood up, almost obediently.

"Perhaps some other time," Angela said to Mrs Murphy, "I might see you when I'm in town."

"A pleasure," said Mrs Murphy, "a pleasure." Already she was looking across to some people at the other end of the restaurant who were waving to her and whom she obviously knew. Mrs Mallow suddenly felt faint: after all Mrs Murphy knew the town better than she did and had other friends: she was only one among many, and the thought laid a heavy grief on her mind. How could one step into the middle of a town and be part of it? It wasn't so easy: in fact it was extremely difficult. For instance it was very odd that Mrs Murphy had been speaking to that abominable Donaldson woman: she should have had more delicacy than to do that.

And as she left the restaurant her last sight was of Mrs Murphy rising from her table and with her duck-like walk, carrying her coffee cup over to where the group of women were sitting and laughing. It seemed as if a key had been turned in a lock: Mrs Murphy didn't belong to her at all, it was only part of her that she knew, and deeper than her relationship with Mrs Mallow was Mrs Murphy's knowledge of and commitment to this small town and her other friends. Bloody Catholic, she muttered to herself, with your talk of your sons, one of whom is probably not a manager at all. Bloody Catholic with your replica of the Manger and the Irish donkey and the green vulgar Irish shrine.

When she turned to Angela there were tears in her eyes.

"A remarkable woman that," said Angela, "she can teach us all."

"Teach us nothing," said Mrs Mallow, and she felt a healthy terrible anger so that she could have gone at that very moment to the railway station and left the town forever. "If she can do it I can do it," she said to herself. "Bloody Catholic." And then, "Anyway her house isn't as good as mine, and she doesn't even have a garden."

4

THE FOLLOWING AFTERNOON (she had decided to leave on the next day after that) Angela suggested that everybody go for a run in Tom's car and have a picnic. "Anyway," she said, "Chrissie will enjoy it and so indeed will we all." And this was what they did, driving through the autumn landscape, the trees on both sides of the road having lost their leaves, the houses silent in the ripe yet slightly chilly light, the streams pouring down the mountainside: and once not far from the road they saw a pheasant, perfectly contained in its own Elizabethan colours, a stained-glass bird, a courtier at a bare court superb in its exquisite array.

"How beautiful," breathed Angela, "stop the car. I wish to look at him." Tom brought the car to a quiet halt and they all sat there gazing at the pheasant which now and again lifted its tall neck and stared around it with aristocratic hauteur as if it were aware of its own stunning brilliance emerging out of the landscape with its fallen leaves and sharp stubbly fields.

Vera in particular stared at it with her own secret smile though she didn't speak to her mother much, now and again regarding her with an almost disdainful look as if she were tired of her incessant chatter.

After they had driven for some time Angela said, "perhaps we could stop at this little bridge. We could go for a walk into the woods just for a short while. Vera could come with me and you, Tom, and your mother could take another direction and then we would pool our discoveries. Wouldn't you like that, Chrissie?" Vera glanced at her mother with undisguised fury but Angela chose to ignore her and they got out of the car and went their ways in pairs as she had suggested.

"We will meet here in an hour," said Angela, clearly enjoying her role of director. "Come on, let's synchronise watches. Isn't that what they do in all those films which have John Mills in them?"

"Sometimes Trevor Howard," said Tom laughingly, but he did

134

as Angela suggested as if it were all a game that nevertheless had to be taken seriously.

He sensed in an inchoate and unfocussed way that Vera's mother was with instinctive intelligence creating a drama of her own and that all of them in this drama had their exits and their entrances, that she was plainly engrossed in her role of producer, partly for its own sake but also partly for the creation of some chosen result: and he wasn't at all deceived by the apparent spontaneity and flamboyance of her gestures for he knew that below them was a deeply serious and perhaps unhappy woman who hung on to the joys of the world as to a raft in the middle of the sea. Thus as he entered the wood with his mother, accepting the production as for the moment at any rate plausible and, truth to tell, willing to be relieved temporarily of the undirected motions of his life, he felt the glimmerings of an unavoidable destiny as one sees at the end of a pathway in a wood the whitish mists of autumn only half penetrated by the sun.

After they had walked into the wood in silence among the dapple of sunlight and shade, Angela and Vera finally came to a glade in which were stumps of old trees and many boulders and stones. There Angela halted, breathing heavily as if she had been making a greater effort than she could easily endure.

She sat down on one of the stumps and then said abruptly to Vera:

"Well, now, what's going on? Your phone calls, brief and dutiful as they have been, suggest that something is going on."

Vera looked down at her with a disdainful smile and answered: "All that is going on is that Tom's mother is with us."

"I see. And you don't like that. Do you mind if we stop here for a while?"

"You don't need to act with me, mother. I know the play from the inside."

"Of course," absently. "Of course. You don't like me much, do you?"

"Not very much."

"I see." She gazed at a buzzard that had settled on a branch, its wings folded.

"What you choose to forget, Vera, is that I've believed in allowing people to grow up in their own way."

"Which is simply another way of saying that you don't care for them. Which is simply another way of saying that you can't be bothered with their runny noses, whether their shoes are polished or not, or whether their tiny minds have thoughts of their own."

Angela sighed again, pulling her red cloak about her as if for greater warmth.

"You're very bitter really. You're not very likeable."

"I'm as likeable as I'm allowed to be. I am what I am."

"I seem to have heard that phrase before but it may have been in another country."

Angela paused as if she were thinking deeply. "You don't really know much, do you? You talk and act as if the world were everything. You're very naïve. Why should it be me you choose to blame your inadequacies on? Has it never occurred to you that you are responsible for yourself? Did you for instance tell Mrs Mallow straight out that you didn't want her in the house. Did you have the guts?"

"I did it for Tom. I thought it would be all right, but it hasn't been. I did what I could. It isn't my fault."

"But when you found out that the arrangement didn't work did you tell her directly. Did you?"

"No, I didn't."

Angela gazed at her daughter as if some inner confidence in her voice puzzled her, as if there was some part of the circumstances that didn't fit.

"I know what you would have done," she said at last. "You would have smiled and kept silent. Have you ever considered that some day you may be in the same position as Mrs Mallow yourself?"

"I'm not stupid, mother."

"Have you considered then what this may do to Tom and to your marriage, forcing him to get rid of his own mother?"

"I have considered all that, strangely enough."

"I see. You're taking great risks aren't you?"

"I'm not taking risks. I'm accepting life, as perhaps you've never done. You married my father to get out of your so boring house as you call it but you don't love him, do you? Well, I love Tom. We were happier before she came than you are with my father."

"Yes, perhaps you were. But perhaps at the cost of shutting life out. Is your life style necessary, may I ask, necessary to you so that you won't run the risk of losing Tom? I notice that you have few friends."

"We have all the friends we need," said Vera waspishly. "If we needed more we would have them."

"Perhaps Tom is your child," said Angela as if thinking aloud, letting her thoughts run on. "The one you never had. His mother was a threat, was she?"

"She was not a threat. She insisted on associating with unsuitable people."

"I see. Unsuitable people."

From her stump of old wood Angela gazed up at her daughter, "Would you consider me for instance unsuitable?"

"I didn't consider you at all, for the reason that you never considered me. And anyway what you've just said is . . ." Vera came to a sudden halt as if she had decided not to say what she had intended to.

There was a sudden whirr of birds about them in the bare wood and at that moment Angela as if for the first time realised that she was not a mother confronting a daugher but one woman confronting another and the pain pierced her heart so that she had to clutch the stump on which she was sitting for support. She felt a dizzying darkness about her.

"I have considered everything that needs to be considered, mother," Vera continued evenly. "Tom loves me. I know that, and that is all I need. I have worked it all out. It is very simple."

"It sounds monstrous to me. But perhaps I am old fashioned."

"Perhaps you are. I know what I want and that is the difference. I am not going to be an ageing actress who speaks her lines to a man whom she finds intolerably boring and whom she doesn't love. I don't find Tom boring. I love him. I am capable of that. And no one shall come between us." Her fierceness was as strong and direct as the descent of the buzzard on its prey.

"I see," said her mother. "It's clear enough. I am confronted by the representative of a new generation, simple, uncomplicated, genuine. And unashamed. The new adult. May I ask you again

137

why you keep that doll in your bathroom now that you are so mature? It occupies pride of place on top of your cistern. I wonder why."

"There is no particular reason."

"Can you not remember where you got it?"

"No I can't and it doesn't matter."

"Well, I can. It's a doll that you once stole from another girl when you were a child. You were at a party and quite blatantly you stole the doll. The mother came to me in great distress because her own child was crying for the doll. We managed to get another one for the child because you refused to give the original one up. No wonder you can't remember. It has blue eyes just like your own."

"You may do what you like, say what you like, but I shan't change my mind about Tom's mother."

"I see."

They stared at each other and Angela knew that her daughter hated her, that somewhere along the road she had been responsible for what was now happening. The world was endlessly complex and justice was unerring and true. She wished that she could say the word that needed to be said but couldn't think what it was, and with a start realised that Vera wouldn't have taken her in either if she had been in Mrs Mallow's position. And at that moment she wished to be back home, with her husband, watching him as he sat in his armchair smoking his pipe and reading the paper. In truth he was all she had: the rest was theatre and nonsense. The new road glinting and hard was too sharp-edged for her: truly she didn't understand it. Truly she couldn't comprehend the risks her daughter was taking so open-eyed and clear-sightedly. My poor Jeff, she thought, we are together in the world, we have no one else.

Suddenly she stood up and said, "Well, that's that then. There's nothing more to be said. Perhaps we should get back." They left the glade in silence and in silence waited at the car for the other two to appear out of the wood. Now and again Angela would make as if to speak but then stop as if anything she said would be useless. It was almost as if she was frightened of her daughter, of her pure natural feelings, for they could be considered in a sense to be natural. They could be considered to be courageous, all those eggs, blank and staring, in the one basket, all those fundamentally sterile eggs.

And she saw her daughter again, withdrawn and pensive, hunched over a book in her room, the doll at her feet, and she said to herself over and over, "Please forgive me O God please forgive me for what I have done." And she would pull her red theatrical cloak around her for warmth.

5

THE OTHER TWO had also in an uncomfortable silence walked into another part of the wood which was not unlike the one that has already been described.

After a while Tom said, "She does go on a bit, doesn't she?"

"I don't like her very much," said his mother.

"Oh? Why not?"

"I think she's deep. She's never had to suffer as I had to. She's never had to live in a tenement. She's always had good things about her."

"That's true." And then consideringly. "But I don't think she's very happy."

"She's got her husband."

"Yes,"

The wood was very quiet with hardly any sound except for the rustle of their shoes over the fallen leaves. The death of the year, thought Tom, that is what we are in at. Not a coronation but an abdication. A sorrow that pierces the heart.

"It's not easy to bring a boy up in a tenement. Many a time I had to keep you from the others. They used such bad language. Do you remember that?"

"Not really."

"I went to the headmaster about you once and he said that you would do well. He said you were a very responsible boy with a good head on your shoulders."

"Did he?"

Their words fell hollowly into the silence as a stone falls down an empty shaft.

At that moment they emerged from the wood and in front of them they saw a lake unruffled and calm. A flock of geese flew high above them in wedge-shaped formation and Tom knew that they were migrating, heading for warmer lands, their necks outstretched as if already they were in sight of it.

He loved the autumn to excess. There was no other season to compare with it. In the autumn there was a sense of slow inevitability as of a world maturing to its proper and exact end. The animals, the birds, accepted it, the leaves put off their array. A brown month majestic in its going, in its surrender to circumstance, putting away its crowns as a child its toys when it is finished with them. Around them some of the colours of the trees were red, some golden and some brown. The season hung at its turning point, like a clock about to strike, waiting, measuring its moment.

The two of them stood beside each other in the wood looking at the loch, he in his yellow jersey and black trousers, his pale face thin and haunted and slightly sad, and she in her black coat and black hat. And it seemed to Tom as he gazed around him that he and his mother were part of a landscape that had existed before they came and would exist after they had gone but that at the same time their lives like those of the leaves were a growing and a fading. He felt it as an almost holy moment and would have turned and told his mother what he felt but he couldn't, for he knew that she would not be able to understand. There was so little really that he could talk to her about: all that bound them together was blood and obligation. He had in his mind transcended her long ago. He was the mountain tall and towering and she was the distant reflection sleeping in the loch. "We have nothing," he thought, "but the natural bond of our blood and bones." His thoughts were not her thoughts nor her thoughts his. All the time he had to make allowances for her: it was an unnatural situation.

"It's beautiful, isn't it?" he said.

"Yes." And then, "How long did that woman say she was going to stay?"

"Another day, I think."

The moment had passed and he no longer felt anything.

"I didn't take to her at your wedding," his mother continued. "She hardly spoke to me. And sometimes I think she looks down on you too. She thinks you're not good enough for her daughter."

"Oh, I don't think that's fair, mother. She's been very nice to me. I know she goes on a bit but deep down she's not bad. She's got a good heart."

"Deep down she looks down on you," his mother insisted. "I know that. You're blind. Just like your father. You don't see

141

things. But I'm too old in the tooth for that." And in her black coat and hat she seemed suddenly fierce and formidable and real.

"Well, all right, then, mother. Perhaps she does. But it doesn't bother me."

"It should bother you then."

She was speaking to him now as she had done when he was a boy, as if he still belonged to her, as if she were telling him to brush his shoes, wear a clean shirt and clean trousers. But of course he didn't belong to her now and he knew that he didn't. If only she would consent to be what he wished to her to be, totally amenable, able to get on with Vera, with no rebelliousness or pride of her own. But of course life consists of rebelliousness, of bristly pride, of flags of vanity. Perhaps she had enough left to live on her own. Enough of pride, which was what it came to in the end.

He turned and looked at her and her face was set like that of a stone image, like a profile on a coin. Absurd in her conspicuous black, a being of nature and yet not of it, she attracted all the more his pathos towards her.

"Anyway," she said finally, "I have my own house. I'm not dependent on her."

They walked slowly from the loch through the trees past the fallen stumps, the stones, the brown leaves, and stood for a moment looking at the car beside which Vera and her mother were standing, slightly apart, not speaking. This is my wife, thought Tom, to whom I must cleave, on whose behalf I swore an oath in church. On that day she had worn white as now, her veil had blown slightly in the breeze, when the photographs were being taken, she had turned and looked at him with love. The minister had spoken, music had played, they were together, two people, separate from all others even from their parents. Outside the church the middle-aged women had been waiting as if they were searching in the two of them for something that they had forever lost: and little boys had scrambled for pennies in the April day of shuttling light and shade. And there after all had been the two of them emerging, nervous and parched, the deed accomplished. There hadn't really been a miracle for the middle-aged women who had turned away as the black taxi left in a shower of confetti like falling snow. There would never be a miracle, only the conjunction of two lonely people in a world that continued on its way as it had always done. And now a little distance away there was Vera standing with her mother, her back turned towards her, the car behind them, and behind that all that the hills. Only another scene that rolled remorselessly from the eternal camera as time passed.

And suddenly as they approached, Angela broke the silence saying excitedly, "Do you think we could have our picnic soon, if dear Tom would drive on a little further to a more suitable spot."

"That's all right with me," said Tom and waited till the others had got into the car before easing himself into the driving seat. They had been driving for a while down a more winding road than the ones they had hitherto encountered when Angela shouted, "This is just the place here, don't you think?" Tom brought the car to a halt by a large stretch of pale dry grass with a loch on the westward side of it and a small stream and fence on the other.

He manœuvred the car on to the grassy verge so that other vehicles would be able to pass and got out, the others following Angela who had the kettle and teapot in her hand while Vera carried the bag with the cups, and sandwiches and sugar and milk and tea. His mother stood about, not quite sure what she should be doing.

"Now then," said Angela again the organiser and director, "I will tell you what we will do. We shall first of all gather some branches and then a circle of stones. Oh, look at that, do you see him? Over there among the reeds."

They looked but couldn't see anything and then she shouted excitedly. "It's a divine little duck and he's peering out at us. He's camouflaged by the reeds. Don't you see his head, the poor little shy thing?" And then they finally did see the duck, hiding behind the reeds, its head peering out from between the green stiff bars and gazing at them. Across their faces passed a slight breeze as if the wind was beginning to rise.

They spent the next few minutes wandering among the trees at the side of the road gathering branches for the fire, Tom breaking them across his knees in order to make them small enough. Finally they had made a reasonable pile which they laid down beside the ring of stones that Angela had arranged.

"You may go for a walk if you wish," she told them grandly. "I shall prepare the tea for you. That will be my work for today."

"Are you sure you will be all right?" said Tom glancing at the dry pale grass.

"Of course I shall be all right. This is not the first time I have built a fire. You go and see what you can see."

They left her bending over the circle of stones, her red cloak flaring and burning in the dry sunshine, as if it were itself a flame that she had coaxed out of the day, and walked along the side of the road next to the trees. They strolled in silence and finally stopped by the loch which was sharp and green with reeds and in which they could see some ducks swimming, and once a large white swan, bent down into the water drinking, its white rump high in the air, its beak deep in the water. Beyond the loch and in the distance they could see a farm with two horses cropping grass in front of it, one white and one brown.

They had been standing there for a little while in the autumn silence when Tom suddenly sniffed and said, "I think I smell smoke" and turning instinctively towards the place where they had left Angela he saw that there were little fires springing up in red rings around her and that she was waving her hands and shouting at them, though they had been so immersed in their gazing that they hadn't heard.

Tom immediately ran back, Vera following him, and his mother walking last.

When he arrived at where Angela was standing in the middle of the rings of flame he saw that the grass, pale and dry, had caught fire in various places, as if the growing breeze had cast sparks here and there away from the centre.

"What are you doing?" he shouted in panic, sensing already that a conflagration was on the way, that the Fire Brigade would have to be sent for, that the flames might spread so rapidly that they would devastate the whole countryside before they could be put out: and indeed they could very well have done that, for the separate burning rings were becoming more and more numerous and searching for union with the others.

He began to jump into the burning clumps and stamp on them with his shoes but as he almost managed to extinguish one ring another sprang up fiercely to his left or right.

"Don't be frightened, "Angela was shouting. "Isn't it beautiful? Isn't it lovely? Where's your sense of adventure?"

And on the outer rim of the scattered fires he saw Vera and his mother, both watching, and neither making any effort to involve themselves though he could see his mother wringing her hands helplessly and Vera coolly gazing as if she were saying to herself, "What a stupid woman. What else could one expect of her?"

He jumped from clump to clump stamping fiercely, grinding his shoes into the flames whilst at the same time leaping away from them in case he got singed and shouting to Angela, "What the hell did you think you were doing? This fire will spread for miles. We should phone the Fire Brigade." And he had visions of men in yellow helmets descending from a red engine spraying water from their hoses while their leader took his name and those of the others and said, "You can't even walk in the countryside without making a nuisance of yourselves." It was the inefficiency of the whole episode rather than its danger that irritated him.

But Angela not at all perturbed was dancing among the red rings crying, "It will go its own way. Fire will take its course. Isn't that right, Vera?" she shouted. "It will go out eventually. Enjoy it while you can."

And in her red cloak joyous and free and seemingly irresponsible as if it were all a show that she was presenting for their benefit she leaped among the flames that she had created, her face almost as black as a gipsy's, while on the edge of the fire Vera stood disapprovingly glacial and remote saying nothing except that once she shouted to Tom, "Come back from there or you'll burn yourself."

And the fire began to roar around him as he stood in the middle, stamping and dancing, thrusting his foot into a flame and then withdrawing it and feeling the stink of smoke in his nostrils till a surprising thing happened and in the heat and glare he suddenly felt free and abandoned as if he had yielded to the fire's power, as if since there was nothing that he could do about it and his efforts were having so little effect (for all around him sprang the remorseless living rings) he might as well let it rage recklessly and maliciously around him.

It was then when the fire was at its fiercest, the breeze whipping it to a peak, that Vera perhaps suspecting that it had become a phenomenon more dangerous that she had expected ran towards him and began to drag him away.

"What do you think you're doing?" she shouted angrily. "Come back. You will be burnt. Come out of there. Will you come back? I'm going to send for the Fire Brigade." And she pulled furiously at his sleeve.

"No," he cried in a rapture of abandonment. "No, we'll stay in the middle of it. It's an adventure."

"Will you come out of there?" Vera insisted pulling at him but he couldn't follow her. "In that case," said Vera, "I'll stay with you."

And she too began to jump up and down stamping the fires with her shoes, her face turning red in the light, with spots of dirt from the fire on it, her white dress losing its purity: so that the two of them were jumping up and down in the middle of the rings of fire, dancing and shouting at each other, as if they were prancing round Angela in a primitive form of worship, while on the outside of the ring the unconsidered Mrs Mallow stood passively suffering what she was unable to do anything about.

The fires sparked and hissed all around them, the light flashed from face to face, their shoes singed and black felt hot on their feet and as if intoxicated by the fire they danced and shouted while Angela answered in a gibberish of her own, improvised it almost seemed for the occasion, and for the first time for many months Tom felt light and free as if he were willing the fire to burn and destroy, to gather its power and annihilate everything in its path.

Suddenly in the middle of the conflagration he began to laugh and Vera looked at him in amazement till she began to laugh too, her face red and dirty, and Tom shouted, "It's all right. How stupid we all were, apart from Angela. She knew all the time, didn't you?"

"What are you talking about?" Vera shouted above the crackling of the flames, grasping his hand tightly.

"Don't you see?" he shouted, "there's no danger. The fire is going towards the loch and on the other side of it there's a stream. It's safe enough. It'll burn itself into the water." He looked back at the burnt blackness of the grass behind and forward to where the fire was burning though less furiously now that it had reached the marshy ground bordering on the loch on one side and on the stream on the other. Hand in hand with Vera he left the centre of the fires to find Angela standing beside his mother and talking to her. When the two of them arrived Angela turned abruptly from his mother and said, "It's all right. I knew it was all right all the time."

And so they stood there watching the fires burning themselves out, spluttering exhaustedly as they met the moistness, till they were finally all extinguished, and only a black waste lay across the ground over which they had travelled: and Tom felt a deep sadness as if some virtue had gone out of him.

"How did you succeed in doing that?" he asked Angela at last.

"I couldn't have made the ring of stones tight enough and then the breeze strengthened," she replied unabashedly. "Anyway you enjoyed the adventure and don't say you didn't."

He didn't answer her and then Angela who had been looking for a handkerchief to wipe her face said, "I seem to have lost my handkerchief. I must have dropped it."

She left them and walked out into the scorched area where the grass had all been burned and bending down began to search.

"Maybe it was burnt," said Tom as he and Vera began to search as well.

It was while investigating the bank of the stream that they found the frog, completely scorched and black, its limbs stretched out. Tom touched it delicately with an exploratory finger and it jerked convulsively.

"It's alive," he shouted to Vera. "Look. It's still alive. Quick. Let's take it to the stream."

Very carefully he who in the past would have been content to look without touching gathered it in his hand, its body, like a miniature foetus, black and scorched and twitching slightly. He placed it on a wet stone in the middle of the stream but it remained motionless. He touched it delicately again and each

147

time it made a faint movement under his hand. Vera watched intently and then suddenly shouted "Be careful." She was gazing with an obsessed fixity. Then very delicately she tipped the frog into the stream and it lay there moving its limbs feebly, still alive, a rough black star. "It will live," said Tom, "it will live." He and Vera had their heads together and as he was about to rise to his feet she touched his arm urgently and said, "Wait, I want to see if it will swim." They watched and slowly, slowly, it began to swim, it began to move its limbs in the water. Without raising her head, Vera said, "Tom, I'm going to have a baby." He gazed at her uncomprehendingly in a dazzle of darkness and was about to speak when she said, "Don't tell the others. Don't tell them. Pretend that I haven't told you."

At that moment as he squatted beside his wife, whose white dress was flecked with black spots and whose face was red and dirty, and at the same time as he watched the frog gathering power in its scorched limbs in the water below, he felt as if he were in a dream, as if he couldn't believe that what he had heard could refer to him. It was as if her announcement drawn out of her by the frog's struggles must relate to someone else, so that he almost turned his head to look for the stranger to whom she was talking. Suddenly it was as if the whole sky, the whole earth, changed, as if there settled on him a weight of responsibility like a stone cloak, as if among the extinguished rings of fire he saw a new world. Clamping his lips together he took her hand and they walked towards the car.

"Well, I'm afraid," said Angela unrepentantly, "that I've lost my handkerchief and my little experiment went wrong. We shan't have any tea either, though I'm sure you enjoyed yourselves. It's the little unexpected things that make life so interesting."

They stared at her in astonishment, she was so determinedly unaffected by her own clumsiness, she seemed in fact to revel in it so much, she was not in the least ashamed or embarrassed and indeed she said, "We must accept the stray chances of life, my dear children. If that fire hadn't occurred we would have had a boring day which we should not have remembered. In any case we may eat our sandwiches." And they sat down on the bank of the road and ate them and Tom gazed at his wife as if seeing her for the first time, as if she contained within her both a hope and a threat, and yet at the same time the inexplicable remorseless thrust of life. He felt on the sandwiches the tang of smoke, the taste of the fire itself.

When they eventually got back into the car, she said with an effort, "I think we should go home now. There's a breeze getting up anyway and it will turn cold."

They drove back the way they had come very slowly as if Tom for some reason of his own were showing the countryside for the last time. After the hectic flurry of flames the trees seemed calmer and stiller, the lochs clearer and bluer, and the silence of the autumn day more present and insistent. They saw birds flying about the sky as if they were preparing to migrate and some perched on fences and telephone wires, their feathers trembling slightly in the breeze, their small heads already turned towards the lands that they would soon inhabit. There were bodies of rabbits on the road, squashed red and raw and flat, by travelling cars, and here and there were also the carcasses of seagulls.

Once they had to stop for a while in the middle of the road to wait for a crow that had alighted on the body of a rabbit and was pecking at it, raising its shining head now and again and looking around with a blank stare. Tom had an impulse to go out and throw a stone at it, as if he felt something obscene in its innocent feeding, and would have done so but that it reluctantly rose of its own accord from the ravaged rabbit whose guts he could see hanging out.

"Oh, look," said Angela, "there's the train," and sure enough it was the four o'clock train winding among the brown hills, heading away from the small town towards the city. Tom refrained from looking at his mother who was sitting beside him, her hands clasped in her lap.

All things continue, he thought, all things continue, but now they will continue in a different way. And he felt sadness as well as joy as if a world to which he had once belonged had come to an end. When he drew up at the door of the house he helped his mother out and then Vera. His mother couldn't leave now anyway, she would have to wait till she got her house back, but in the end she would go, especially now. He had had to make a choice and now a new one was being made for him. It was a choice between Vera and his mother and, anguished though it was, life demanded it. There was no going back to a world that had once been and he must learn to swim in the new world. Thus as he steered his mother into the house it was with a tenderer touch and as he looked at Vera it was as if he knew that whatever she was, in her fierce love, he had chosen her and must abide by her, for that very possessiveness must have been one of the reasons for his love. Astonished by this revelation he stood for a moment dazed in front of the door before entering so that Angela had to speak to him as he fitted the key into the lock and even Vera herself looked surprised by his absentmindedness.

Finally, however, he opened the door and let them all in one after the other, and then followed them, and it seemed to him that the house itself had changed and become a sort of shelter against what was to come in its unpredictability and its strangeness.

PART FOUR

It was a day in April when Tom and Vera took Mrs Mallow down to the railway station to see her off to Edinburgh. Unstated though understood, the departure had been in their minds for a long time, but when Tom woke that morning to see the glare of light about the bedroom the imminent parting had returned to him as a shocking surprise: and yet it was not as if he wouldn't see her again. Breakfast had passed in a silence that was almost meditative: and now they were at the railway station staring at the train that was waiting at the platform. To Tom it was as if the train were bearing both his father and his mother away from him: Vera on the other hand reposed in the sluggish triumph of her future. The two women regarded each other from inside a world that Tom did not understand, as if they had learnt a wary respect each for the other. They briefly kissed and then Tom took his mother's case and walked with her to the door of a carriage that was already open. He swung the case on to a rack and then helped his mother aboard. She said, "Look after yourself," and he muttered some reply. It was as if he wished it to be all over, and indeed it seemed that his mother too wanted to leave and be back in her own home, in its independent silence. "You don't need to wait," she said, but he waited just the same, not speaking, just being there: there was little that he could profitably say. Then he saw the dingily-uniformed guard with his flag, in his moment of importance. There was a piercing whistle and he stepped slightly away from the train, seeing his mother in black standing at the window, diminished and distant. The train began to move, to shudder backward and forward as if reflecting the motion of his own mind. Then it gathered power and decisiveness and started on its way. It was as if he could see the rails narrowing and widening, narrowing and widening, a complex metallic loom. His mother wasn't waving, she must have gone to her seat. He walked back past the barrier to where Vera was waiting, her large belly outthrust, slightly sleepy and satisfied. He did not look her straight in the eye but began to walk with her to the exit from the station. As they did so and as they passed the bookstall they saw, as if it were in a strange vision, as if it were fated, Ruth Donaldson standing there turning over some magazines and it seemed to Tom that they were the magazines of sexual fantasy that the schoolboys were always studying in their furtive groups. As they passed she looked up and it occurred to Tom at that moment to go over and speak to her, to say that he held nothing against her, that life was what it was and that no one could be held responsible for it. But Ruth Donaldson was gazing at his wife's triumphant body, swollen as if under sail, and he could not fathom the expression in her eyes. It might have been the utmost fever of despair, it might have been a perverted reflected triumph of its own. It was as if she were on the edge of a feast that she envied or despised, he couldn't make out which. At any rate as he made a slight move towards her she deliberately and unsmilingly looked down at the magazines again, as if she were withdrawing into the reality and limits of her own life. And yet he felt her burning, scorching, ugly and present. For a moment he thought that she was what Vera might have become, and he suddenly took his wife's hand as if she had had a narrow escape in front of his eyes. His mother in black speeding through the countryside to her home and Ruth Donaldson standing at the railway bookstall were part of the one vision: they were on the rim of his world. His hand tightened on Vera's, warm and frail: and then the two of them left the railway station and made their way to the car. Ruth Donaldson had not lifted her head but appeared absorbed in the magazines, and it occurred to him that perhaps they had only been a refuge for her from Vera's tremendous glow. The seagulls on the pier were still pecking at the herring bones and one of them yawned vastly, its yellowish gullet visible. The sea glittered extensively, light flashing from it in all directions. On the hill directly ahead and above him he could see the trees, with the leaves beginning to tremble on them. Already the spring could be felt in the air, naked and vulnerable. He opened the door of the car for his wife, eased himself into the driving seat and they set off home.